THE DAY I LEFT

JASON KOROLENKO

THE DAY I LEFT. Copyright © 2012 by Jason Korolenko. All rights reserved. No part of this book may be used or reproduced in any manner whatsoever without written permission except in the case of brief quotations embodied in critical articles and reviews. For information address the author at www.jasonkorolenko.com.

Second Edition, MightyRed Publications.

Cover design by Jeroen ten Berge.

Author photo by Scot Wilson for FlickerLight Photography.

Interior format and layout by Jason Korolenko.

ISBN-13: 978-0615737348

ISBN-10: 061573734X

For Mom

I always said the first one would be for you.

PROLOGUE

BUT HE DOESN'T SPEAK to me anymore.

Stephan Gerardy sets the pen down, presses his palms hard into his eye sockets. When the blast of static in his vision fades away, he notices dried ink in the webbing between his right thumb and forefinger. The joints in that hand ache; he'd spent all morning on the final report. Six months' worth of details, six months since Jarrod, withdrawn and unspeaking in shock, had begun writing his story, passing pages to Gerardy as he finished them. Sometimes, in a frenzy, the kid would write several in a day. Other times, weeks would pass without a single word committed to paper.

Six months, Gerardy thinks, sinking into his chair. *Has it really been so long?*

He reads that last sentence—*But he doesn't speak to me anymore*—three times, as if such close scrutiny will reveal some new, hidden layer in the story. He glances over at the empty chair beside Jarrod Nelson's bed, and he sees Jarrod staring at the chair with something like patient expectation.

"That is it, then?" Stephan asks in a voice seasoned with Spanish accent, though he'd lived on the French side of the border his entire life. "This is the end?"

Very slowly, as if he has collected all the time in the world and will dispense it as he wishes, Jarrod says, "I don't think I've left anything out."

Stephan nods. "They've convicted the bartender,

Monsieur Nelson. Attempted murder. We informed him that a self-defense plea was invalidated when he made a conscious decision to grab his baseball bat and continue chasing you after you left. He accepted the charge in exchange for a lesser sentence."

"So what about me?"

Stephan shakes a cigarette from a half-empty, crumpled pack, and slips it into his mouth. Of course he notices the sign on the wall, the one that reads *Il n'est pas permis de fumer.* Of course he isn't going to light up in a hospital. In fact, he'd quit the habit several years ago, the very day his mother died of lung rot.

But the taste of an unlit cigarette is still divine.

"I'll come back tomorrow," Stephan says, sliding the pages—a couple hundred of them in total—into a leather briefcase. "We'll talk more then."

Jarrod says nothing. He simply returns to staring at the empty chair, suppliant, as if waiting to be told what to do next.

Stephan thinks he may be waiting a long time.

ONE

I WOULD HAVE DONE anything for Caroline. Know that. The way she reached up, tied her burnt auburn hair into a messy knot, and gave me that look; that one with eyebrows raised in something between expectation and disappointment.

That's where it all started. With that look.

"He's very protective," she said, "and he's met hundreds of guys just like you, Jarrod."

Pierre, she meant. Her brother. Also my sociology teacher at the university in Pau. The one who grimaced and shook his head every time I opened my mouth.

"When your term is up," she went on, the English words slippery on her tongue, "you'll go back to America and forget all about me."

"How could I forget you?" I said, reaching for her chin. Caroline evaded, sat back and crossed her arms.

"But you'll go back."

"I don't know about that."

"What would you do here? Your French is terrible."

I mirrored her posture, a playful gesture. In response, Caroline leaned forward and blew out the candle on our table.

"Who cares what your brother thinks?" I asked, frustrated. Trying not to sound desperate.

"He's my *brother*."

"Not your father."

She sipped her wine, a cheap red from Blois instead of Bordeaux because that was all I could afford, and glanced up the road. A bicyclist blurred by, leaving in his wake the sound of hard rubber tires rattling on cobblestone. We were outside, a patio table at some Italian restaurant near the chateau where Henri IV was born—the infant king's newborn body caught in a turtle shell, according to local legend—with the Aquitaine sun setting on a decidedly unromantic evening.

"I'm telling you," she said, twisting her fork into fettuccini, "you have to make friends with him."

"That's it? That's your big plan?"

Caroline dropped the fork, drained the rest of her wine. Covered the mouth of the glass when the maître d' passed.

"You've heard about his new project?" she asked.

"He doesn't talk about it much in class. And my French is awful, remember? I don't understand half of what he says."

I'd been in the country for almost six months, the first half of my junior year of college, and had barely moved past the basics of communication. Even with Caroline as a language tutor. *Especially* with Caroline as a tutor. Her lips kissed words in a way that made it hard to concentrate.

"He has this obsession with gang mentality," she said. "He goes on and on about how groups of people act differently than any of the individuals would independently."

"They egg each other on," I said.

"No. Like they develop a separate consciousness." She waved this off as if it weren't important, then said, "He goes to bars, really dirty, nasty places, and takes notes as everyone gets drunk and belligerent."

I laughed, imagining Pierre in a corner booth, half shaded in low light, wiry John Lennon glasses sliding down his nose as he watched and wrote. Almost hiding, not because he didn't want to be noticed, but because that's just who he was. Private, like his sister. He'd be wearing a tweed jacket with black tie underneath—always overdressed at school, much more so for a lower class pub—still smelling of roses or oleander or whatever fancy eau de toilette he'd settled on that day.

"It's not funny," Caroline said. "I'm afraid for him."

"I'm sure he knows what he's doing."

"Haven't you noticed?" she asked, eyes pinched into almond shapes. "Don't you pay attention? You saw him on Monday."

Monday. I'd come early to class that morning, after running laps around the campus to burn off a mild hangover. It was unusually cold for June, crystals of dew spread out over the lawn like a shiny white blanket. When I first saw Pierre doubled over his desk, he was popping painkillers and washing them down with mineral water.

"And I swear he was wearing makeup," I said, laughing again. "Concealer or something."

"He was beaten up the night before."

I felt my face go slack.

"I told you it wasn't funny," Caroline said.

"I hope he got all the notes he needed."

"It's happened before." She removed the pin from her hair, shaking curls loose over her bare shoulders. "It won't stop him."

The first time I had seen Pierre outside of the university, I was preparing to board the train after a weekend of tourism in Lourdes, a Catholic mecca about an hour's ride away from Pau. There, disembarking, was Pierre with his crooked smile and bulbous cheeks, pulling a wheeled suitcase behind him and fingering a silver crucifix around his neck. I was sure he'd noticed me, though he turned away as if he hadn't. The second time, a few weeks later, we'd crossed paths at L'Opera in Paris. I had been training at a martial arts academy up the street, he'd been watching an adaptation of Hugo's *Les Miserables*.

"*Comment tallez-vous?*" I'd asked him.

He'd responded in English, looking everywhere but at me.

"What can I do for you, Monsieur Nelson?"

Caroline had only recently told me Pierre was her brother. I wondered if he knew about us. Not that there was an *us*, romantically, at that point, but I had been pursuing her for weeks. Flirting during our language sessions. Meeting her downtown for drinks. Following her like a dog on a chain.

"Nothing," I'd said. "Just saying hello."

"Hello back." He'd smiled, but I couldn't tell if it was genuine or if he was humoring me. "You enjoy the city?"

"Very much. Better than Pau, that's for sure."

"Pau is, how would you say, a bit rough around the edges?"

I'd nodded. "Someone stole a payphone on campus. Ripped it right out of the booth."

"Hooligans."

He had closed his eyes, shaken his head as if the deed upset him greatly. Just as I'd decided to change the subject, to talk to him about my feelings for Caroline, he shook my hand, told me he'd see me in class, and walked off.

"Pierre has a dark side?" I asked Caroline now. "I never would have guessed."

"He doesn't advertise."

"So what do you want me to do?"

"Go with him tonight, but don't tell him I sent you."

"And why would I want to do this?"

"Don't sound so indignant."

"I think you mean facetious. Or flippant."

"Don't sound those either." She reflected my smile at her choice of words. "Just talk to him like you're interested. And if something happens, you can help him."

"That's why I don't go to bars. Something *always* happens."

"Even better. When you rescue him with your *martial arts expertise*," she said in a teasing tone, "he'll owe you a debt of gratitude."

"A debt of gratitude? Who talks like that?"

"Don't make fun of me," Caroline said, smiling wider and exposing a few too many teeth.

"Let me tell you a thing or two about men."

"I'll bet I know men better than you."

I reeled back in mock surprise. "I'm going to pretend I didn't hear that, you slut."

The pink tip of Caroline's tongue made a brief appearance.

"Listen," I said. "Men don't like to be rescued." Caroline's gaze broke from mine, and the sudden good humor drained from her face. "We'd rather take a beating than allow someone to come to our aid," I continued, turning to see what had grabbed her attention.

"He's right, you know," Roger Watford said, cruising up beside me and laying straight for that innocuous European cheek-to-cheek kiss on Caroline, a greeting that never seemed very innocuous to me. At least not when it came from Roger.

"It's emasculating," I said, narrowing my eyes at the back of Roger's head and thinking how badly I'd like to emasculate *him* at the moment.

"What are we talking about?" Roger asked, piling his Australian burr on thick. "Or who, should I say?"

"Nothing important," Caroline said. "In fact, we were just about finished."

"It's lucky I saw you here then," Roger said, "because I locked myself out of the flat again."

I frowned, reminded of Caroline's insistence that they were just roommates. No matter how platonic she claimed they were, I envisioned her in a flimsy, see-through nightgown, curled fetal on the couch and chatting it up with Roger in front of some cheesy old movie. They'd be speaking in French, of course, because he was fluent and I wasn't.

The fucker.

"You'll talk to him, then?" Caroline asked me.

Roger transferred his weight from foot to foot, looking quite like a little boy in need of a piss.

"I'll talk to him," I said.

TWO

STANDING OUTSIDE THE ADDRESS Caroline had given me, I understood why the bar went unnamed. This was the type of place that did not want to be found. There were no advertisements, no windows, just a tall, skinny door in the middle of a blockhouse on a street barely wide enough to drive down. I hesitated, searching for any signs of life, even pressing my ear to the worn, unpolished wood and listening for curses, laughter, the clink of glassware. But there was nothing, only the low roar of a televised soccer game coming from up the street. A sudden wind blew over a metal trashcan. A cat screeched in a nearby alley.

The door opened and an Algerian man practically fell out. The stench of pastis rolled off of him so thickly I could almost see it clouding in the night air. He looked up at me with blank eyes, pulled his mustache, and stood aside. The hallway from which he'd come stretched back about twenty feet. Bare red bulbs hung from the ceiling, gently swinging from thin metal chains and doing little to mask splotches on the wallpaper.

"*Entrez-vous?*" the man asked, holding the door with one hand, laying the other on my forearm.

I twisted into him, acting without thought, slapping the hand away as soon as I felt its touch. It was a natural reaction, like catching a ball or slamming on the brakes when a kid runs out in front of your car. Years of training will do that to you.

9

Paranoia will do that to you, too.

"*Poutain,*" the man said, raising his arms in supplication, then stumbling off.

I caught the door before it closed, slowing my breath, strangling down a surge of adrenaline.

This is a bad idea, I thought. Places like this weren't friendly to foreigners. Places like this weren't friendly at all. But Caroline's silky voice crept into my ear, saying we could never be together if I didn't gain her brother's trust and respect. And if that weren't enough to push me through the door, imagining her with Roger Watford was.

I followed the hallway to a T-junction, now able to hear voices and muffled music. *Je Ne Regrette Rien*, I recognized, that old Edith Piaf song about how she regretted no part of her vulgar, whorish life. To the right, a cracked open door with the letters WC hung askew. To the left, another short passage opened up into a room obscured in white fog.

Smoking had been outlawed in public establishments the year before.

The blood began to rise again in my wrists.

Everyone in the room turned to have a look at the intruder. There were couches lined up along the far wall, coffee tables with hookahs belching out puffs of smoke and bleary eyed onlookers behind them. Film posters from the forties or fifties, their corners torn, black-and-white pictures yellowed with tar. An old style jukebox, and hunched over selecting tunes on the machine, a bulky bald man wearing a black leather jacket. He watched me with particular interest, squinting, as I entered.

I felt pinpricks of attention, their judgmental eyes scanning me from head to toe. It seemed as if all activity, all sound—the jukebox music included—stopped when I came in, even though I knew that was just my perception. I stood frozen for a moment, like an actor performing on stage for the first time, paralyzed under spotlights and scrutiny.

"*Qu'est-ce que tu veux?*" the bartender asked. He leaned

forward with both hands on the bar, muscles in his arms elongating beneath dark brown skin. He addressed me informally, which could have signified either lack of education or lack of respect. I noticed a metal baseball bat propped up behind him, its handle wrapped with electrical tape, and decided on the latter.

"I'm looking for someone," I said, scanning the room for Pierre. "*Je cherche quelqu'un,*" I repeated, hoping I chose the right words, hoping the bartender understood me. At the sound of my classroom French, the smokers went back to their hookahs, the drinkers to their drinks, the bald man to his table, all unimpressed with this short, skinny foreigner.

I had that small element of surprise in my favor, at least; I didn't *look* like I could fight.

"You'd better look with a drink in your hand, *American*," the man said, "or you can get the fuck out."

I spotted Pierre sitting at a booth in the corner, just as I had imagined, on a blackened pew that looked like it had been rescued from a cathedral in flames. He dipped his chin, pretending not to notice me. That old game we all used to do as kids: *If I close my eyes, you can't see me.* He pulled deeply from a cigarette, whistling smoke from his lips and inhaling back through his nose.

"Did you hear me," the bartender asked, "or do I have to speak up?"

I cleared my throat and ordered a Stella Artois. He poured the beer into a dirty glass. I thought it best not to fill out a comment card.

Pierre saw me coming and sighed, breathing out so heavily he seemed to shrink a couple of inches. He removed his glasses, wiped the lenses clean. The ghost of a purple bruise was still visible on his left cheek, curving gently away from the arch of his nose. In his blue and white striped polo shirt, two days of shadowy growth on his chin, he looked more casual than I imagined him capable.

"What are you doing here?" Pierre asked. He had a

notebook with him, a notebook he quickly folded closed when he caught me looking.

"Caroline told me you'd be here."

"Of course she did."

"It's not what it looks like," I said, sitting beside him, against the wall, because I hated the oppressive breath of a crowd at my back.

Pierre raised his eyebrows, sliding his glasses back on. "What does it look like?" he asked.

I shrugged, reminding myself to take the beer slow because I sensed a long night ahead, but inhaling a third of it like a professional drinker.

"What did she say?" He mimicked Caroline's raspy, high-pitched voice. "*Buy him a beer, Jarrod. Make friends with him.*"

"Word for word." I smiled, trying to scale the wall of disgust he was building between us.

Pierre snorted, drained his glass, and waved for another.

"I'm not going to hurt her," I said.

"Ah," Pierre pointed to the ceiling, his accent thickening exponentially with each drink. "You don't *intend* to hurt her, you mean."

"I mean what I said."

I knew this wasn't going to end well. Looking back on it now, if you asked *how* I knew this, I couldn't say exactly. But as the other patrons watched Pierre and me with peripheral, suspicious glances, and as the bartender—who Pierre referred to as Brick, possibly because of the man's burnt brown skin color, but more likely because he looked like he was carved out of stone—watched me with particular interest, I felt my fingertips start to rap nervously against the tabletop.

The record in the jukebox changed, an erratic, static-filled hiss as Edith Piaf became Elton John.

"Look around you." Pierre pointed, slipping into professor mode, and openly drawing the attention of a few of the skinhead's compatriots.

I couldn't decipher the whispers coming from that side of the room, couldn't tell what language the guys were speaking or if they even understood us.

Pierre went on, his voice growing louder in his prosthelytizing. "At least one of these men—more likely three or four—will go home tonight and hit their wives or children. Or both."

"I'm sure the alcohol has something to do with that," I said, the irony not lost on me as I finished my first and ordered another.

"What I'm saying, Jarrod, is that we hurt people. We don't always mean to, but we hurt people. It's what we do. It's coded in the DNA."

"You have an awfully cynical view of the world outside the classroom."

"Oh, we're not all sociopaths," he said, accepting two new glasses with a nod and sliding one to me. Brick slipped a receipt under Pierre's ashtray, and there were at least seven there already. "However, though we may feel remorse afterward, this does not mean we won't cause pain again in the future."

"So you come to places like this to confirm what you already believe?" I shook my head, matching Pierre's pace, sipping when he sipped, pausing when he paused.

"It's a microcosm," he said, only now beginning to slur. "A test subject, *une petite société*, where I can watch a dramatization of the downfall of man in one evening." Pierre smiled, a dark and stubbly version of that same toothy grin Caroline showed whenever she was worked up. "And it happens *every* evening. It's fascinating."

The record changed again, from *Goodbye Yellow Brick Road* to The Doors, fading into a thunderstorm backdrop with an ominous keyboard melody laid atop it.

I took a slow drink this time, using the opportunity to better gauge our surroundings. A few of the patrons scowled, the obvious eavesdroppers, one even leaning over and spitting on the floor. The bald man, though, was my main concern. Judging simply by his aura, by how he sat confident and upright like a soldier, by how the others shut up whenever he was talking, I suspected he might become a problem. But no matter how well trained I was, I knew that groups of people never attacked one by one like they do in the movies. In real life, fights were complete chaos. It was like facing a multi-headed beast, all punching and kicking and hair pulling and biting—without discretion—at anything that moved.

"I think we should talk about this somewhere else," I said. Someone nearby replied, in English, that it would probably be a good idea.

"I'm not finished with my beer."

"Yes, you are," the bald man said, pushing up from his table, approaching with lips twisted and fists clenched at his sides. His jacket was unzipped, and intuitively running scenarios, I figured I could choke him with his own lapels if I had to. "Beat my wife and kids?" he said. "How about I beat *you?*"

"Come on, Pierre," I said, laying out the euro for unpaid drinks.

Pierre stood, wavered, nearly tumbled over. I caught his arm, threw it around my neck and dragged him toward the door. He sank his weight like an insolent child, trying to take me down with him. He had spoken clearly enough to fool me. I knew he'd been impaired, but until he was on his feet, I hadn't realized how drunk he really was.

"I'm sorry for him," I said to the bald man, and to Brick, and to the few others who had gathered, all brimming with hateful energy.

No one opened a path as I maneuvered toward the door, but no one stopped us either. I avoided their gazes, focusing instead on Pierre. Making eye contact with someone who only wanted to drink, fuck, or fight wasn't a show of confidence. It was a challenge. For a moment, one painfully short moment, I actually thought we might get out of that bar unharmed.

But then Pierre turned his head and shouted something in French, something I didn't understand. Time slowed down and the atmosphere grew humid with the threat of impending violence.

I blinked, and that was all it took. A shot of lightning rocked my head forward, this vicious burn on my skull as warm liquid soaked into my hair. On the floor at my feet, shattered glass, beer and blood swirling together. Testosterone in the air like pit-stink.

In a daze I hurled Pierre forward and instinctively thrust my foot backward, feeling it sink into someone's gut.

Brick hopped over the bar, twirling his baseball bat.

Fuck me, I thought, panic rising in my chest.

"We're leaving," I yelled, one hand up in surrender, the other covering the back of my head where the pain rolled in like crashing rain from the jukebox. *Riders on the Storm*, still playing, but nearing the end. I guessed it had taken five minutes, tops, for the situation to spiral into chaos.

I walked sideways to provide a smaller target, but also so I could keep one eye on Pierre and one on the others. Most of the patrons hung back, cursing, but tentative now that I'd struck back. Even Brick let us go, grimacing, but seeming content now that we were on our way out.

But the Alpha Male, the leather-clad skinhead couldn't let it end there. There was always one, a thoughtless brawler who would continue to lash out just for the sheer pleasure of fighting, of dishing out pain, who would relight the fuse after cooler temperaments had allowed the fire to die.

He tried to dive past me, reaching for Pierre, but I reacted before he did and caught the back of the man's jacket, using his own momentum to trip him onto his face. I grabbed Pierre's wrist and pulled him toward the hall.

"I'm sorry," I said again, so anxious to just get the fuck

out that I felt tears stinging my eyes.

Brick helped the man up, but held him back when he tried to follow us.

My ear throbbed and rang, my vision blurring as I pushed Pierre ahead of me through the hallway. I hoped there wasn't any glass stuck in the back of my head. I kept turning back, this horrible mounting fear over me, like when I used to stay up late without my parents' permission to watch *Tales from the Darkside* with all the lights out. Even when we hit the street, the main door closing behind us and shutting the threat inside, I still felt that fear breathing down the back of my neck. I dragged Pierre a couple of blocks before he finally yanked from my grasp and dropped down to the pavement, gasping like he had just swum the English Channel.

"That was a close call," he said. In the moonlight, his red face looked sinister, sweat sticking the clothes to his flesh.

I gently laid a palm on my sticky scalp, wincing at the burn.

"But we have to go back."

"Are you mental?" I asked.

"I forgot my notebook."

"Listen to me," I said, squatting down and grabbing the collar of Pierre's shirt. "We're not going back for your goddamned notebook. You're going home. To bed."

He laughed. A jagged, harsh and derisive sound that made me want to hit him.

I'm not proud to admit that.

"Are you going to babysit me?" he asked. "If not, I'll just go right back after you leave."

"That's your choice. But I'm taking you home. I owe Caroline that much."

Pierre looked up, a flash of fury screwing up his face. "You *owe* her?"

"She's worried about you." I held out my hand. "Get up."

He struggled to his feet, pushing me away and righting

himself, balancing against a chain link fence that separated the street from a construction site, a row of condemned buildings with metal scaffolding running up the sides.

"She's afraid to tell you the truth," Pierre said.

"The truth?"

He didn't say anything of value after that. Just nonsense. I let him lead the way, trailing behind a few feet in case he stumbled or fell, but he already appeared to be moving steadier. I wasn't familiar with the area, knew that we had turned off of Rue Marchand a couple of blocks ago, but kept a mental note of landmarks in case . . . well, just in case.

I saw him to the door of his apartment, where he disappeared inside without even a thank you, his only goodbye the sound of a deadbolt clinking into place after he shut me out. An upstairs light came on, his silhouette moving slowly behind a shuttered window. Then the light blinked out and that was the last I saw of Pierre.

"The truth," I mumbled, sitting down on the curb, pacing back and forth in my mind, my heart still racing.

I flipped open my cell phone to call Caroline, tell her Pierre was fine—if a little pissed off—and ask her what the hell he'd meant by *the truth*, but the screen was gray and unlit. Dead battery. Again. I considered stopping by her apartment on my way back to the dorms, but it was late, must have been nearly midnight. And the state I was in, I didn't know how I'd react if I knocked on her door and Roger answered it. I didn't trust myself.

"Roger." I tasted his name, rolling it over and over again on my tongue, wondering if he'd been through this routine, too. Had he gained Caroline's trust by making friends with Pierre?

I sat there for a few more minutes, waiting to see if Pierre would make good on his promise to go back for his notebook. Inspected my palm, damp and sticky from holding it against the wound on my head. I wiped some sweat from the back of my neck and saw that it wasn't sweat at all.

When I finally stood, my equilibrium went haywire and I fell back down, dizzy and seeing white noise. Like when we were kids, and Mario Nunez and I would sit with our heads between our legs, forcing ourselves to hyperventilate so when we rose up quickly, our blood pressures would plummet and we'd black out for a few seconds, just long enough to have visions and dreams that seemed to last for hours.

The sounds of sirens in the distance brought me back around. I pulled myself up, slowly climbing from my mental fog, and went straight home to avoid any further trouble. Charged up my phone while I showered. The faucet sputtered in cold bursts, barely enough pressure to clean the dried blood from my head. Pink rivulets trailed down my skin, backing up in the drain as the water always did, leaving me standing—leaning against the tile wall—in a shallow pool of thinned blood. Every muscle in my body felt like it had been hammered into submission and *God* there was so much blood still rinsing out of my hair.

When I stepped out of the bathroom, drying myself with an off-white and frayed towel left behind by some other student, a red light on the phone was flashing. Someone had left a voicemail. I keyed in the pass code, expecting to hear Caroline's voice, but got my mother's instead.

"Jarrod," she said, sounding stretched tight like a high wire just in the mention of my name. "Your father's had an accident. It's serious. You have to come home."

I was on a train by one in the morning, boarding with groggy families eager for their weekend trips to Paris. Lightly packed and cautiously optimistic, armed with the number of a flight that would leave that afternoon, I silently prepared my apology to Caroline, hoping I'd be back soon, and aware that I had done exactly what she'd expected.

I'd left.

THREE

WE ROLLED INTO GARE de L'est, brakes screeching out a violent wake-up call, commuters and tourists already jostling into line and fighting for their luggage before the train came to a complete stop. Roman numeral clock towers on the landing announced our arrival at seven-twenty. I had to be at de Gaulle by noon to make my plane. The stench of oil and hot metal rose off of the train tracks as we all descended like children excited to be out in the world.

I shouldered through the masses, ignoring the newspaper boys and the indoor cafés with their steaming containers of coffee and warm, freshly baked baguettes, trying—and failing—to quiet the cries in my stomach but continuing on anyway, and headed for the escalator that would take me down into the belly of the station, down to the TGV line that traveled direct to Charles de Gaulle airport.

On my way past a row of low hanging plasma televisions, I caught the tail end of a breaking news report from Pau. By the time I heard the town's name and found the screen from which it was coming, the scene had changed to show images of newly detonated bombs in some Middle Eastern country.

School probably shut down again, I thought. It had been happening off and on for the past month, students blocking the doors from the inside with chairs and overturned tables, protesting a government bill that proposed privatization of all universities. A week earlier, it had gotten out of hand. Police showed up, tore down a bunch of red banners painted over with black fists. Rocks were thrown. A couple of kids had to be transported to the hospital, and a couple more were arrested.

But as much as I wanted the news to be about the school, or about a visit from President Sarkozy, or about plans to divert traffic during the upcoming Tour de France, something tossed my guts when I thought about Pierre and our adventures from the night before.

Breaking news reports from Pau were rare, mostly because little of importance ever happened there.

After sleeping off the alcohol, would he appreciate what I did? Or would he reason that nothing would have even happened had I not intervened? I supposed there was some logic in that thought. After all, it was my mention of Caroline that had inspired Pierre's diatribe about violence and abuse.

And what would he think, come Monday morning, when my seat in his sociology class was empty? What would he think on Wednesday, when I missed a second class?

I knew I'd have to report my absence to Malcolm McCormack, the study abroad director, but I made a mental note to ask Caroline for Pierre's number so I could talk to him directly. After what we went through, the thought of speaking to him so soon made me want to vomit, but if I planned on any kind of a future with Caroline, it had to be done.

But what to tell Malcolm? What to tell Pierre? My mother hadn't gone into much detail in her message, only that Dad had fallen from a ladder—probably a few Tecates deeper than he should've been—while working on the roof. Severe bleeding in his brain. Doctors said the first few days were critical. If he made it a week, chances were he'd recover. If he didn't make it, then he didn't make it.

But I couldn't entertain that thought. Couldn't even accept it as a possibility. That my father was hurt, sure. That he might die within forty-eight hours? I was numb to that reality.

Much of my time that morning languished in distraction. Reflecting on it now, I have only fleeting memories of passing through airport security, finding my gate on time, every minute or so checking my cell phone, and even continuing this habit after the juice in the damned thing drained out again. I wondered if Caroline was sitting at home —Roger sleeping in and snoring like an obnoxious drunk— waiting for me to call. I wondered if my mother would try to call again with worse news. My ticket back home was one-way, open-ended. I wondered how soon I'd be able to come back.

And I wondered how long before Caroline asked me to babysit her brother again.

My flight to JFK with a connector to Phoenix was scheduled to board in just over two hours. I grabbed a sandwich and a demi bottle of wine, found a secluded corner to plug in my phone, and as soon as the device powered up, it rang.

"Mom?" I answered.

She was crying, and the sound caused a hitch in my own throat.

"Mom, what happened?"

"You asshole," she said. It took me a few seconds to realize it wasn't my mother who'd just called me an asshole. It was Caroline.

"I'm sorry," I said, the script of my mental apology vanishing. "I meant to call you earlier, but my phone wasn't working."

"God, you are such a bad liar."

"My father had an accident, Caroline. I'm going home."

A woman's voice, robotic and lifeless, came over the intercom system, announcing boarding calls in several different languages.

"Where are you?" Caroline asked, sniffling, adopting an accusatory tone.

"Paris. My flight leaves soon."

"That was quick."

"My mother bought the ticket. I had no choice."

She laughed then, this stutter of disbelief that shot barbs through the phone. "You're such a fucking coward."

"I'll come back as soon as I can. It won't be—"

"You said you'd protect him." The sobbing picked up again. "You promised."

"Caroline, what are you talking about?"

"My brother, you shit. How convenient that you are leaving now."

An invisible hand reached out and plunged into my stomach. "I put him to bed," I said, remembering Pierre's insistence that we go back to the bar for his notebook. Did he return alone, after I'd left him? Did he get beaten up again?

"He's dead, Jarrod. Do you hear me? Pierre is dead. My brother is *dead*."

FOUR

"YOU'RE SO PALE," MY mother said, pressing a sandpapery hand to my forehead.

I grew up in the desert, usually sported a year-round tan. Of course I'd be pale after six months away. But everything grew hazy after we picked up my luggage and stepped outside, as if the atmosphere were some great vacuum that sucked all the moisture from my pores. The July heat hoisted me up with sinewy arms and threw me to the pavement. Mom put me in the car and headed toward urgent care.

But the heat wasn't my only problem. It was just another added shock.

"How's Dad?" I asked, the words dripping slowly from my lips.

"He came home today."

"Is this a joke?"

"Why would I joke about this?"

I resisted the urge to raise my voice. In truth, I probably didn't have the energy to. "You made it sound like he might die. If he's home already, he must be okay."

She didn't respond. My mother had a tendency to overreact, to place universal importance on the smallest things. To complain about how rough she had it, when she probably had it better than a lot of the other mothers I knew. She once burned a pan full of brownies she'd been baking for a dinner party. She canceled the party, cried herself to sleep that night, and then avoided her friends for weeks out of embarrassment.

"Why are we going to the hospital, then?" I asked, feeling duped and too angry to discuss Dad's condition any further.

"For you."

"I'm fine."

"You're *not*."

"Why isn't Caroline with you?"

"Caroline who?" she said, laying a palm on my forehead. "My God, Jarrod, it feels like there's fire under your skin. And what the heck happened to your head?"

I'd meant to say *Jeanette*, not Caroline, but a thick liquid foam seemed to have been injected into my nervous system, clogging up the hoses between my brain and mouth.

I certainly hadn't expected Jeanette to be waiting at the airport, swimming her way through the crowd, waving a pink handkerchief in slow motion as the escalator brought me down to her. Unlike my mother, who had reluctantly accepted my decision to spend a year studying abroad, Jeanette viewed my departure as a personal affront. We spoke a couple of times while I'd been away, but the gaps between the calls and emails had become wider each time. When we did talk, we both sounded distant, an audible chasm in the phone line that hummed and filled the awkward silences.

Riding shotgun now in my mother's rusted out, wood paneled station wagon with a collection of magnetic Jesus fish on the back, everything was the same, but nothing was. We blew past the Circle K where Mario Nunez and I got drunk for the first time, slugging Mad Dog 20/20 by a fat green dumpster behind the building. A mirage, vanishing into a bright flash of sunlight. I shielded my eyes, squinted, thumbed my temples in an effort to dull the pains that shot around in my skull like a pinball. Saw the La Caruna complex where I kissed Gina Moreno in one-fifty-two, a dark and abandoned apartment roped off with caution tape. She moved away shortly thereafter, before I could make it to second base.

Jeanette had been my first double, triple, and homerun.

The apartments shimmered behind a haze of oil and then disappeared. We veered onto the highway, rows of cacti and ashen bushes on either side of a road that led straight into the deceptively distant mountains. Mom ran the air conditioner on full blast but it didn't help. Exposed skin still stuck to the leather seats, the inside of the glass still burned to the touch.

I focused on the dumbest things. A pulsing green gecko skittering into a dime-sized hole in the sand. My mother's nose hairs flittering in and out as she breathed. Liver spots on the backs of her hands. The urban clusterfuck of Phoenix shrinking into the rearview mirror as we escaped into tiny, desert neighborhoods.

Thinking of anything but Pierre Coudreau.

Dr. Goshen was concerned by my inability to sweat. Dehydration, most likely, me unused to such arid extremity and clinging to the last few drops of water in my body. She put me on an IV drip, said I could die if I tried to rehydrate by quickly drinking a lot of water. I overheard her say something to Mom about a fever, about how I shouldn't leave until it broke.

"And what happened here?" the doctor asked, parting my hair and inspecting the damage from a couple of nights before.

"I fell."

"You've got a pretty decent gash. It's clotting, but not closing. I'll stitch it up and order an MRI for good measure."

I sat in the hospital room for a couple of hours, dozing in and out, lulled by the steady drip of the IV. Listened to the woman one room over complain about an STD she'd contracted in Colorado. Mom on the pay phone down the hall, checking up on Dad, informing him that we'd be late for dinner.

"How is he?" I asked when she came back in. Purely out

of frustration with her, I added, "Dead yet?"

She narrowed her eyes. "That's not funny."

It wasn't, and I was sorry for it, but I didn't tell her that.

"His filter's gone," Mom said.

"What do you mean?"

"You'll see. I'm tired, Jarrod."

As if I wasn't.

I slept most of the way home, a heavy, drug-induced listlessness during the two-hour trip south to our rundown border town on the skirts of Mexico. I dreamed a little, unable to keep Pierre from creeping into my subconscious, a fresh corpse lying facedown on a cracked, unkempt sidewalk outside of a nameless bar. The type of street with metal cages protecting the windows. Cigarette butts collected in the drains like cockroaches. Blood on the pavement, spilled from somewhere inside Pierre's blue and white polo shirt. His John Lennon glasses no longer perched on his nose, but at his fingertips as if he'd reached out with his last effort, grasping for his vision so he could see who had done this to him.

Night had fallen by the time we arrived. I fought through grogginess, nausea, and jet lag to haul my bags inside, where Dad lounged on an old velour sofa Mom had bought at a yard sale at least a decade ago. He sat upright, listing slightly to the left, staring at a blank television screen. The same rabbit-eared RCA they had moved out of my bedroom when the bulbs in our last television blew. Nothing had been updated while I was gone, though Dad himself had apparently downgraded. For the most part, he looked fine, which made me want to curse my mother, as if she had consciously tricked me into coming home when I should have been in France with Caroline. Dad even sat in the dark, shades pulled tightly closed, as he always did when he drank. But now there was a Pepsi in front of him instead of a Tecate.

"Hello, Jarrod," he said, and then I realized he was *not*

fine. He gave me a once over with his right eye, while the other stayed aimed at the blank television. "Where the hell have you been?"

"France, Dad."

"No kidding." He cocked his head, appearing genuinely surprised.

"You drove me to the airport when I left."

"You're joking."

"Can you still see out of that thing?" I asked, pointing at the drifter.

"Well enough to tell you're an ugly bastard. You got your father's looks." He laughed, cackled really, then turned back to his non-existent program.

On the surface, things had changed. Deep under the skin, the skeleton remained the same.

In my absence, Mom had stuck a batch of glow-in-the-dark stars on the ceiling of my bedroom. I dropped my luggage at the foot of the bed, scanned for Orion and the dippers, the only constellations I knew. Cassiopeia always sounded more like a Greek sandwich than a cluster of stars.

"Were you planning to rent my room out to traveling toddlers?" I asked.

"I thought it might feel more homey," she said. "Like the sky is always the same no matter where you go."

"It's a nice idea." I climbed up to peel the stickers off. "But I'm twenty-three, not twelve."

She lowered her head, swept away uneven bangs she always cut herself. "Are you hungry?"

"Sorry," I said, absently picking at the bandages on my head. "It's been a long couple of days."

"Can't I bring you something?" She stood in the doorway wringing her hands together.

Dad shouted from the living room. "Marion, the goddamned TV is busted again."

"You have to turn it on, sweetie," she said.

"Get in here and show me your tits."

I couldn't help but smile. "No filter," I said.

"No filter." Mom smiled back, red blush blooming in her cheeks like cherries. "They said there might be some problems with his impulse control."

She left me to unpack, but I pulled out my laptop and surfed to the BBC website, finding the European news link and clicking on the little pentagon-shaped map of France. Buried in the list of headlines—TGV strikes, soccer scores, sexual controversies among high-ranking political figures; you know, the usual—the title, "University Professor Murdered In Pau." I held my breath, tapped the trackpad, and waited for a video box to open.

The clip began with a stock photo of the school, the Maison de l'Etudiant building just across the street from my dorm. A few students milled about in the picture, a circle of beautiful people sitting cross-legged in the absurdly green grass beside the parking lot. The doors of the cafeteria open wide. Faces caught in mid-laugh, but I doubted anyone was laughing now. Strange to see the place again, in that capacity, this otherwise quiet town as a focal point for such a horrific crime. The image switched to a portrait of Pierre, smiling his off-kilter smile, peering at the camera through a pair of wire-rimmed glasses.

"Coudreau was found dead," read a newscaster, this one riding on an uppity English accent, from off screen, "early this morning, by a local shopkeeper on Rue Marchand."

Rue Marchand? That was nowhere near the bar. Or Pierre's apartment. When we'd turned off of Rue Marchand that night, we'd run at least two blocks before stopping.

How long? I wondered, my chest tightening as a pair of tears slipped down my cheeks. *How long did he wait before going back out again?*

Details, the reporter said, were forthcoming. She mentioned nothing about a sheaf of papers or a notebook, only that Pierre had no wallet on him when the body was found. Suspected mugging gone wrong, authorities suggested.

I knew better.

Dad appeared in the doorway as I started to draft a message to Caroline.

"How are you doing, old man?" I asked, wiping my face.

"Better than you, it seems."

"What happened? Mom was vague. Skimped on the details." I started writing—*Dear Caroline*—only looking at Dad in the reflection of my computer screen.

"I got beat up. At the bar."

"That's awful," I said, typing *I feel terrible about Pierre.* Not immediately registering that Dad's story didn't mesh with what my mother had told me.

"I thought you fell from a ladder?" I said, distracted by Dad's image shimmering in the computer screen, a splotch of red on his t-shirt catching my eye.

"I did something stupid," he said.

I twisted to face him, my fingers stabbing out letters on autopilot. He wore a blue and white striped polo shirt, untucked. No red anywhere on it. I focused again on the screen. Not only did there appear to be a splotch, but a glare of light drew wire thin glasses on my father's reflection.

My father didn't wear glasses.

I closed my eyes, pressed my palms into them. *You're overtired,* I thought. *Stressed. Seeing things that aren't there.*

"You could've helped me," he said, "if you had been there." Dad's voice had a slight upward tilt to it, the shadow of a foreign accent. "You and your *martial arts expertise,*" he added, sounding awfully like Caroline, at the Italian restaurant a few days before, when she'd said essentially the same thing.

"Martin," my mother said, tugging Dad's sleeve. "The doctor said you should be resting."

As she pulled him away, my father winked with his good eye, the floater seeming to linger and scan the letter I was writing to Caroline.

* * *

Sometime in the middle of the night, unable to sleep under heavy thunder and monsoon rains, I got up and checked the news. The Internet browser was still open to the BBC site, my unfinished document minimized at the bottom of the screen. I could apologize to Caroline a thousand times over, but would it matter? Had she already condemned me as a failure, unable to protect her brother and thus unable to protect her?

Worse, I envisioned Roger Watford in her ear, feeding her anger and influencing her opinions of me. Saying things like, *Every martial artist I've ever known has wondered what it's like to really put the hurt on someone.* Asking things like, *Why do you think he left so suddenly?* Brushing his fingertips along her thigh, using her vulnerable, sorrowful state to slide further into her heart.

Another article on the BBC page, another picture of the university in better times. Around five-thirty on Saturday morning, it read—when I was dozing on the train a couple of hours south of Paris—a patisserie owner on Rue Marchand had discovered Pierre leaning against her glass door, dead. After police responded, they'd followed a blood trail from the patisserie back to its source, the area where they believed Pierre had been beaten. An area about fifty yards from the door of his apartment building.

I read that part twice, confused, wondering why he would have run *away* from his home.

Authorities suspected Pierre didn't want the mugger to know where he lived, that he was trying to protect his wife.

That hollow emptiness crept back into my stomach. My eyes burned.

Pierre had a wife.

FIVE

I HAD SLEPT POORLY after reading the news that night, even exhausted as I was, just kept replaying those last moments outside of Pierre's apartment and hearing Caroline say *he's dead*, three times, each time more emphatic, like she couldn't quite believe it herself, or like she thought it was my fault. And in those long, early morning hours, that stretch between two and four when the world is so silent you can hear the wind whispering to you, questioning you, breaking you down and making you question yourself, I started to feel like it *was* my fault.

I shouldn't have left so quickly. If I had stayed only a few minutes longer, I might have run into the skinhead and his friends.

They must have followed us.

Dad had an appointment in the morning. The three of us sat at the counter eating breakfast, subdued and quiet. Mom absently picked at a corner of her toast, contemplating the endless expanse of grit and mesquite outside the kitchen window. She hadn't spoken all morning. I hadn't heard from Caroline since her phone call at the airport.

"Can't I have one beer?" Dad asked, using two of his curled fingers like a spoon, scooping his cereal and drooling half of it from the side of his mouth.

It would be funny if it weren't so sad.

The rain had continued on from the night before, rolling through in a magnificent torrent, spraying up sand and filling the air with the scent of cleansed earth. Monsoons didn't normally last that long. Usually they came and went in sporadic bursts, sometimes five minutes a shot, leaving in their wake flooded cattle guards and destroyed roads and a sky so blue it looked like you could swim in it.

"Jarrod," Mom finally said, "you're going to have to drive." She slipped a tiny white pill onto her tongue, choked it down with some orange juice. "This is all too much for me."

"I'll have to go back," I said. "To finish school." School was the least of my concerns, but she didn't need to know that.

"Why don't you wait for the diagnosis." Not a question.

"You told me he fell from a ladder," I said, aware of that mildly spiteful tone creeping back up my throat.

"And?"

"He told me he got into a bar fight."

Dad looked up at me with a sparkle in his eye, a devious glare like we shared a secret that I wasn't supposed to tell.

"I never said that," he said.

He dove back into his cereal so suddenly that I wondered if we really *did* share a secret, or if he'd simply forgotten he'd said it.

"I watched him fall off the ladder," my mother said, shaking her head as if I were a Class A fool. "I was right there when it happened."

We said nothing more about it.

At the hospital, the doctors put Dad through vision tests, cognition tests. They checked his reaction times, scanned his brain once more. He took it all in stride, complaining only when they made him put on the pale green gown that opened in the back to expose his ass. He wanted to wear it the other way. He thought the nurses would like to see his willie.

They released him after a few hours, maintaining that his condition was stable. Swelling in his brain had already gone down, bleeding had stopped. They told Mom to make sure he stayed away from aspirin and alcohol, anything that might thin his blood, and to come back in a couple of weeks if nothing changed before then. Before we left, my mother cornered the doctor to talk him into extending her Xanax prescription. Said with all this stress, she needed it now more than ever.

And again, I wrestled down that selfish fury that she had made me come home for *this*.

When I pulled into the driveway, Dad hopped out—yes, he actually *hopped* out, like a bunny or a kid forty years younger—and went straight to his workshop in the garage next door. Mom, on the other hand, doped up and eyelids heavy, needed my help getting inside. When I came back out to rescue Dad from himself, Mario Nunez was kicking up clouds of dirt in the driveway, booting a soccer ball over and over against the garage door.

"Didn't expect you back so soon," he said.

"How'd you know I was home?"

"How many chicks did you fuck?"

Bang. The soccer ball dented the metal and bounced back from the shivering door. My father, inside, shouted for him to knock it the hell off.

"Those Frenchies don't shave," Mario said. "Do they?"

Bang. He skipped as the ball returned, a fancy step-over maneuver he probably learned from watching Mexican soccer matches on Telemundo, one of only one channel we received that far out in The Nowhere.

"I mean, they like it natural, right?"

I shrugged. He knew he was winding me up. It was a game to him.

"And they stink, too. Don't believe in deodorant."

"That's a myth," I said. "They don't stink any worse than you."

"Calm down there, gringo. I'm just playing."

Bang.

"You seen Jeanette yet?" he asked. The tone in his voice

had changed so subtly that I barely noticed it.

"I'm trying not to."

"Those European girls spoiled you."

"Fuck off."

Bang.

"She asked about you," Mario said, catching the soccer ball on his instep and balancing it there. "How you were doing."

"I wonder why she didn't ask me. She had plenty of opportunities."

"That's not all she had plenty of."

Bang. Bang. Bang. It wasn't the ball those times, but the thud of my heart trying to force its way through my breastbone.

"What's that supposed to mean?"

"Nothing." He shifted away before I could catch his eye, then quickly added, "Just messing with you. So—"

Bang.

"—how much trouble did you get up to out there in cheese country?"

Mario was a bastard. I mean that; he didn't have a father. He told the story to everyone he met, that Papa Nunez knifed a drifter down in Sonora while he—Mario—was but an infected egg inside his mother. During a long and dramatic flight from both Border Patrol and the Federales, a flight that grew longer and more dramatic every time Mario recalled it, the old man jumped from a moving train. Didn't survive the fall. That's what Mario said, anyway. No one really knows for sure. There are a lot of nameless bodies in Sonora. A lot of dead drifters, too.

Mario always said fathers were overrated.

I wasn't about to tell him about my troubles in France. With his mouth, the whole state would know by the end of the day.

"What kind of joke is that?" I said. "You think it was easy leaving Jeanette?"

"You sure made it look easy."

She lived only a few blocks away, across a shallow valley that was our version of the proverbial tracks separating the good side of town from the bad. She lived on the good side, so you can guess where that left me. The valley, littered with empty Mickey's bottles and sun-bleached beer cans and discarded cigar fillings that were scraped out to make space for marijuana, was where the cholos hung out, the gangs, the drug dealers. Jeanette used to find it romantic that I'd brave the skels and criminals gathered in the shadow of the valley of death to see her. They messed with me quite a bit in the beginning, busted my lip a few times before I snapped and started to fight back. I was a white guy in a sea of brown, *victim* all but tattooed on my forehead.

"Almost like you ran away," Mario said, kneeing the ball up, watching it hover and momentarily block out the sun.

I punched it across the yard. "Ran away from what?"

"Surprising, that you of all people don't know."

"Ran away from what?" I repeated, clenching my fists and ready to jump him if he evaded again.

Mario just looked at me, shook his head. He was my oldest friend, but not my best. We'd fought before, mostly over Jeanette, but he'd never been afraid of me.

A loud crash came from inside my father's workshop; first the sound of a hammer on metal, then something like bowling balls dropped through sheets of glass. Then nothing. Then Dad's voice bloated with disappointment. "Ah, Christ."

I turned away, jogging toward the garage while Mario hung back. I pretended not to hear his parting comment, hoped, in fact, that I hadn't heard him right.

But I had heard him perfectly.

Jeanette was pregnant.

SIX

ONE OF MY EARLIEST memories took place in New Hampshire, when I was maybe five or six years old. It was February, and in a flash of brilliance, my father had decided to package the family up and drive some donuts in a nearby parking lot, during a blizzard. Mom had shoved my pink feet into boots that hurt because they were a size too small, wrapped me in a coat with a jagged piece of zipper at the top that scratched my neck, and pulled down over my eyes a fraying wool hat that made my skin break out in an allergic rash.

We climbed into Dad's pickup truck. He insisted we wouldn't need to strap ourselves in, the three of us crammed into the one seat up front, and besides, we were in the "Live Free or Die" state. I can still picture that beast of a vehicle clearly, bright red with chains on the tires, a healthy assortment of dents, and a number of bullet holes riddling the sides. Real bullet holes, shot through when Dad and his friends got drunk and played with guns, not those fake stickers you saw at novelty shops.

I sat wedged between Mom's spongy thigh and the gear shifter, could barely move, and that was likely the only thing that saved me from being tossed through the windshield when Dad plowed into a deer. None of us had even seen it through the thick white flurry. It was like the animal dropped right out of the sky and onto the hood of the truck.

Dad had some burns on the insides of his wrists from the

airbag popping out, Mom had smacked her head into the windshield, leaving a small, bright red spot on the glass. The acrid powder from the airbag choked us up a bit, but we were otherwise okay. The deer didn't fare so well. It was still alive, twitching and making slurry noises as it breathed blood through its broken face, when Dad pulled the shotgun out from behind the seat.

The crash hadn't scared me much. But watching Dad move with such calm assurance to raise the double barrel to the deer's head cramped my bowels something fierce. The animal saw him coming, tried to stand on shattered legs. Its matted, deformed chest still rose and fell despite the broken ribs and punctured lungs beneath. I saw Dad's lips move, but I couldn't hear what he said over the gunshot.

Mom clamped her hands over my eyes a second too late.

Little Jarrod's attention was drawn away from the gruesome sight of a bullet exploding through the deer's face. He was transfixed by the delight on his father's face—a look Grownup Jarrod would describe as orgasmic—the excitement, the burst of laughter that came out when he took the creature's life.

That was the day Little Jarrod learned to fear his father.

When we moved to Arizona after the northeastern branch of Mom's company transferred operations to Mexico, my parents dropped me into an after school martial arts program to keep me entertained. I took to it pretty quickly, mostly because I had nothing else. We lived so far from anything or anyone that the other students in those classes provided my only sense of camaraderie. I wasn't making friends in school —I was the minority, as I may have mentioned. Sat in the back of the bus, hiding by a window, but still frequently spat upon and crushed against the sides by a Mexican with long dark hair, like liquid onyx, while the rest of the kids laughed.

Things were little different at home, when Dad would return after work wanting to test what he called my "ninja skills." I never fought back, even as I grew to be almost a foot taller than him, and stronger, while the only part of him that grew was his gut.

The dynamic in our relationship changed the day I was expelled from school, the last week before summer break, shortly after my fifteenth birthday. The lunchroom was in a building facing the main school grounds, a hundred or so yards of desert field in between. As the year had wound down, gang fights were common in that field. Some days we'd sit in the lunchroom and just watch, a cloud of brown dust obscuring much of the action as twenty or thirty people collided in the middle like a sandstorm. They'd fight with hammers and even knives sometimes, until it became almost a daily occurrence and police were posted at the school. In the morning, they'd be waiting with handheld metal detectors as the buses arrived, patting us all down like we were prison inmates instead of students. They patrolled the grounds at all hours, even recruited willing parents to follow kids around with video cameras.

The schoolyard dustups stopped suddenly, not really because of the police or the parents, but because of the kid who'd accidentally blown his own head off in the bleachers during class. He'd been ditching, passing around a bottle of tequila with his friends, showing off his new toy. He'd removed the clip, jokingly placing the tip of the barrel at his own temple. One of his buddies made the news that night, crying about how he'd shouted, warned the kid about the bullet still in the chamber.

How he'd snuck the gun onto campus, no one knew.

A little over a week before the end of that year, most of our tests completed and lockers cleaned out, the activity started up again. Fights broke out at any given moment, and the town was small, so there weren't enough police to assign to the school grounds. Two guys would start swinging in the bathroom near the gymnasium, while a group of vatos jumped a quiet kid with glasses on the other side of campus. Cops couldn't keep up. Parents couldn't carry enough videotape to film it all.

I was minding my own business. Walking back from lunch, head down, refusing to make eye contact with anyone, when someone bumped into me from behind. I tripped, caught my balance before I fell. Maybe my father had hit me the night before, maybe he hadn't, but the proliferation of violence at school mixed with my problems at home broke something in me. My Zen was snuffed out just like that, a dark moon eclipsing the sun.

That cliché about blacking out when swallowed by complete, mind numbing rage? Totally true. I hit the kid over and over, not realizing until much later that he'd been apologizing for bumping into me, saying some *other* kid had pushed *him*. Raising his arms over his head for protection, not even attempting to fight back.

When the moon passed and the light came back on, the kid was fetal on the ground, crying. I was crying, too. Bawling, actually, because the last thing I ever wanted to do was cause someone else pain.

I wasn't proud of what I did. I'm still not proud. But something good came of it. After they kicked me out of school, and my father heard the story of what I'd done, he never touched me again. Maybe *he* was proud.

Or maybe he was scared.

SEVEN

A COUPLE OF SUMMERS ago, the city raised property taxes on Dad's shop in town. He'd converted our tin-roofed storage garage into a workspace. He'd laid off his entire staff, using me for free in peak summer temps to help him move. We rented a truck, and ended up loading in most of the heavy stuff like tongs and hammers and bags of coal and empty tubs, while Dad attended to business—usually in the form of a sixer of cheap Mexican beer—in the back office. At the house, while we unloaded, he tried to teach me how everything worked, how the vent would have to be angled just right over the forge so he wouldn't asphyxiate. I rebelled. The second-to-last thing I wanted to do with my life was pound steel and sweat and inhale toxic fumes all day. The very last thing I wanted to do was pound steel and sweat and inhale toxic fumes all day with my father.

Reeling and confused by Mario's news, still not wanting to believe that Jeanette was pregnant, I burst through the garage door to find Dad leaning against the hearth, a pair of massive shears in his hands. He looked up at me with a frown, then back down at the shears. He held them over a sheet of metal, but each time he attempted to cut, he missed by nearly a foot.

"I can't get the damned thing to stay still," he said, snapping the shears open and shut. He had already knocked over a table, a shelving unit filled with oils and lubricants and whatever else he used to twist and mold steel, and a fire extinguisher, which was now on its side sputtering mouthfuls of foam from its beak.

Each time Dad thrust the blades downward, he came closer and closer to slicing off his kneecap. Exposed through holes in his jeans, the skin there was already cut and bleeding.

"Goddammit," he said, pencil-thick tendons popping out of his neck. "Stop fucking moving."

"Dad, put the shears down."

"I've got work to do."

"You're going to hurt yourself."

"I'm going to hurt *you* if you don't shut up."

I inched forward, timing my entry, yanking my hands away when they came too close.

With that one eye suddenly focused on me, Dad thrust out, the points of the blades coming close enough to my cheek that I could have shaved with them. He pulled back, and I saw in his expression the intent to strike again. Pain stamped all over his face, a pent-up, ferocious smirk as if he were nothing more than a hateful creature trapped inside the body of a half broken man. I had seen him angry before, had bore the brunt of his drunken fist, but never like this.

This wasn't my father.

I struck his elbow, knocked the shears aside, then circled around behind him and tied up his arms. He struggled only for a couple of seconds, and then went limp.

"What the fuck was that?" I said, sinking my fingers hard into his flesh.

"I couldn't cut the metal."

"So you thought you'd cut me instead?"

"What are you talking about? Mercy, kid. Let go of me."

I released him, kicking the shears across the floor in case he decided to try his luck again, but I could already tell he was exorcised of whatever had come over him. His eyes were *his* again, the floater floating and the other just kind of lost.

"I'm exhausted, Jarrod." He looked around, rubbing at the back of his neck. "Clean this mess up for me, will you?"

I was too stunned to say anything.

On his way out, limping slightly on his left side, he said again, "Mercy."

The door closed behind him. His weak leg dragged in the dirt outside, sounding like a barber's straight razor across beard stubble, and when he passed by the smoky, four-paned window, he turned his head and smiled at me. A crooked smile that was gone before I could blink.

He hadn't said, "Mercy."

He'd said, "*Merci.*"

EIGHT

ONCE HE'D GONE, ONLY then did the tremors start. Hands shaking as I sat and combed fingers through my hair. That gleam in my father's smile when he'd snapped the blades at my face, it was hunger in rictus form. Not a desire to scare, but a desire to hurt. Or, at least, to revel in someone else's pain. Scarily familiar, since I had seen it only days before when Pierre spoke of the wife beaters in the bar, and of how fascinating was their nightly spiral into sociopathic behavior.

Of course, I reasoned, *Dad hadn't said "Merci" when he'd walked out.* My subconscious simply highlighted that specific connection between the two men.

I told myself that. Did I believe it?

But I laughed, and I heard the nervous tremor there, too. I chided myself for even entertaining the thought that Pierre and my father held the same capacity for violence. The laughter faded when I thought about Caroline. I didn't know how close she and Pierre were, but they were close enough that she'd needed his approval to be with me. There would be an investigation. Had she already told the police I was one of the last people to see him alive?

The incident with my father and a pair of shears was the deciding factor. I'd had enough. There was no longer any reason for me to stay in Arizona, while the girl I wanted to be with was in France mourning her brother's death. A death I didn't want to feel responsible for, but was starting to. The radio silence since her phone call at the airport, those last moments on the line before she hung up, the low static still in the back of my mind, sounding like the hum of a bladed pendulum. If she had been disgusted with me for leaving then, what was she thinking of me now? The longer I stayed away, the harder it would be to go back, the more justifiable her damnation of me.

But there was Jeanette.

Mario had left while I was inside dealing with my father, before I could corner him and ask if he'd been joking around again, or if I'd actually misheard him, the way I'd misheard Dad earlier.

I thought about our last night together, Jeanette's and mine, the night before I'd taken a flight to study overseas. We'd gotten drunk, but not *too* drunk.

I had to know.

"You know how much I hate to be alone," Jeanette had said, just before the end. She skipped ahead and faced me. Pushed her palms against my chest. "Why are you avoiding me?"

"I'm not avoiding you. You've been busy at the bakery."

"Don't turn this around on me. I've been calling you every day."

"I haven't gotten any messages," I said, feigning anger. As if it were somehow her fault I'd deleted the voicemails without listening to them.

"Why haven't you called me, then? It's been almost a week."

Almost a week. What had I been doing? Filling out paperwork. Applying for passports and student visas. Meeting with advisors. Listening to those *Instant Conversational French* CDs. Emailing martial arts academies in Paris and Bordeaux and Biarritz.

But did I tell her that? No, not then. Did I tell her I had already purchased my ticket, departing in less than a month, to study in France for a year? No. Did I tell her that Arizona was starting to feel like a black hole, a desert filled with nothingness, a place where dreams went to die? I did not. Because Arizona was *her* place, *her* dream. Born and raised there among the cacti and boulders and mountains and hour-long drives to the closest supermarket, Jeanette felt right. She'd never leave. Even though we'd had conversations about relocating, imagining a life in California or the Midwest or maybe even Canada, I knew she'd never leave.

"Do you think that's normal? Ignoring me for a week after six years?"

She said it as if we were married, as if we hadn't spent the majority of those years breaking up and making up, fighting and fucking, routinely alternating between being sweet and being spiteful.

So, no. I didn't tell her then. But she went back door, the next day, and asked my mother why I was so distant. Mom was never discreet. She loved to talk. She spilled everything, thinking Jeanette and I had discussed it.

"You know how much he loves that savate stuff," Mom had said. "He's already made friends in Paris who practice it."

"Savate? I've never even heard that word before."

A French style of kickboxing. I had told Jeanette about it at least a hundred times, but I didn't blame her. It was my obsession, not hers. She had no reason to care.

Mom told me later that she regretted saying anything. She'd gotten defensive with Jeanette, as a mother will, I suppose. "Imagine how cultured he'll be in a year's time," she told her.

Jeanette took it badly on two fronts. I'd been sneaking around on her, making plans to leave, and then there was my mother's subtle inference that Jeanette somehow lacked culture. We didn't speak for another couple of weeks, but I knew we'd have to before I left.

When it finally came, the conversation was much less

hostile than I expected it to be. But that only made it more difficult. I was prepared for the fight. I could deal with my pain.

I couldn't deal with hers.

"Why can't you stay here with me?" she said. She didn't raise her voice. Wouldn't look at me.

"It's not that I don't want to stay with you." In fact, I wanted to leave that day. I wanted to leave right then, if only because Jeanette's pain was rolling off of her skin in waves, slowly sinking into mine, and I was afraid it might force me to change my mind.

And if I'd stayed, would I have resented her for it?

"Then why do it?" she asked, gnawing so vigorously at her lip that I thought she might chew right through it. "What's the point?"

"The point is I want to do it," I said, perhaps a little louder and more firm that I should have.

"You don't think it's a big deal. Jarrod, it's a *huge* deal. What do you expect me to do while you're backpacking around Europe for a year?"

"Do exactly what you're doing now. Spend time with Mario."

Jeanette turned away, hiding her face. I'd said it before, exposed my jealousy over their friendship. Remembering our old arguments, I saw Mario at the center of most of them, but this time, I didn't mean it the way she understood it.

"This'll be good for us," I said. Of course I felt bad. I handled it all wrong, but I didn't know how to let her down without hurting her. "It doesn't have to change anything," I said, when in fact, I hoped over time, it would just cause us to drift apart, and we could both avoid that final, awful confrontation.

"It changes everything," she said.

And she was right. It had already changed everything.

"The world is a smaller place," I said. "We'll video chat.

It's not like I'm going to Serbia." My stomach was starting to ache. I wanted to console her even though I knew it wasn't right. But if I had, would I have been trying to spare her feelings or mine?

From there the discussion became circular. Accusations of selfishness, excuses that were rooted mostly in that very same thing, all in various stages of despair and hostility. We spent the night before my flight huddled together in a sleeping bag under the stars, sharing a bottle of coconut rum, kissing and crying and fooling around, trying to laugh and fight our way through it, promising we'd come out on the other side stronger than before.

But it was fantasy, and I think we both knew it.

Now, all these months later, I couldn't tell which was the fantasy, France or Arizona. The ground beneath my feet didn't feel entirely solid, like I was walking in a dream, and Pau seemed so far away. Had Pierre really died? Had that actually gone down? It crossed my mind to stay in Arizona, to forget everything else. Over a long enough period of time, I was sure I could even convince myself none of it had happened.

But there was Caroline, and the flipside. If I went back to France, perhaps over time I would forget about Jeanette. Forget about her baby.

The baby.

The building was once a miniature strip mall with two units on either side of a bakery owned by Jeanette's grandmother. A real estate agency—now closed—empty, except for scattered bits of particleboard furniture. An army recruiter's office—now closed—also empty, save for a single poster of a ramrod Marine with a sword at his side, the site transferred to Tucson when Uncle Sam realized the pool of potential soldiers had dried up. An arcade—now closed, bought by someone in town and turned into a storage unit that was frequently broken into. And a small library, now closed because people out here had better things to do than read, like shotgun tequila and beat their kids.

She stood at the far side of the shop, opposite the doors where I entered, an elderly couple blocking my view. But the bob of messy hair sticking up from behind the old woman's cauliflower head was definitely Jeanette's. I could name that topknot in two notes.

The elderly couple parted as if this were a dance choreographed for my benefit. Their hands remained linked, tanned brown arms forming a V with Jeanette in between. Our eyes met; hers were heavy and tired and as beautiful as depression. The elderly couple came together again, once more blocking Jeanette from my sight, and I realized I'd been holding my breath. My hands tingled.

Was I too young to have a heart attack?

I remained beside the door, jaw clenched so tightly that my temples hurt, when the elderly couple pushed past and exited, the old man carrying a cane, the woman a boxed chocolate cake.

"When did you get back?" Jeanette asked after a pause. She stood behind the counter. I couldn't see her stomach from there.

"A few days ago."

"You're pretty white."

"Don't you dare call me gringo."

The threat of a smile. "Mario still calls you that."

"He does."

It was a strange conversation, harmless small talk, made all the more strange since I was still by the door, a good fifteen feet away. Neither of us made a motion to approach, separated as we were by empty space, and fittingly so.

"So you've seen him?" She appeared to struggle with this question, as if she wasn't sure she wanted to ask it.

"I saw him earlier."

"And?"

I lifted my chin. "And what?"

I've never been a good liar. Not even by omission. And she knew me too well to buy my false ignorance.

"He told you," she said.

Jeanette stepped out from behind the counter, a beige apron tied loosely around her waist. A slight bulge pushing the apron out around her lower abdomen.

"How long?" I asked.

"Until I'm due?"

"How long have you been with Mario?"

She dropped her head, strawberry curls falling loose ever her ears. "It's not exactly like that."

"Not like what?"

"You were gone," she said. "What was I supposed to do?"

I imagined myself standing on a cobblestone street somewhere in Pau, a cold June rain spritzing around Caroline and me, a background painted with gold light.

But then Roger is there, materializing like an apparition, standing beside her with an arm circling her waist and a cocky grin on his face. And Caroline saying what Jeanette had just said.

You were gone. What was I supposed to do?

I left the bakery without saying anything more, thinking I might never see Jeanette again.

She didn't run after me, didn't say goodbye.

NINE

WE WERE PARKED OUTSIDE the terminal in Phoenix, the very next morning, Dad in the back seat, seeming to have forgotten he'd tried to deface me the day before. It had been less than a week since I'd been home, but it wasn't home anymore. And every hour I stayed was another hour Roger could use to coddle his way deeper into Caroline's life. I know that sounds petty, considering Pierre's murder and my pregnant ex-girlfriend, but there you have it. Caroline was all I could think about. She was my escape from all this. From traitorous friends and co-dependent mothers and brain damaged fathers.

She was the one real thing I wanted to happen.

"Jarrod," Mom said, "do you really have to do this? Can't you stay a little longer?"

"You wanted him to go in the first place," Dad said. "No matter how stupid it was for a southwestern boy to learn French instead of Mexican."

"Spanish, Dad."

"That too."

I said my quick goodbyes, refusing to linger not to avoid my own sense of sorrow, but so my mother wouldn't wallow in hers. She didn't need another excuse to chew pills like chickpeas. Her husband was excuse enough.

Another airport, another security disrobing, another full body x-ray. A portly woman in line behind me complained loudly about the machine, drawing pinched stares from TSA officials, asking everyone within earshot if they knew just how much radiation was being charged into our bodies when we passed through these things. She'd pause in her rant only long enough to inhale a bite of the double cheeseburger dripping ketchup into her fist.

Radiation appeared to be the least of her worries.

On the other side, waiting to board, I called Caroline, this time staying on the line through the voicemail prompt and leaving the first substantial message since I'd returned to Arizona.

"It's me," I said. "I don't know what else to say, other than I'm sorry. I have no idea what happened after I left."

A voice crept into my head, the low drunken whisper of an imaginary Pierre giving substance to my guilty conscience.

You know exactly what happened.

"He must've gone back out," I said.

I even told you I'd go back for my notes.

"I shouldn't have left," I said, both to myself and to Caroline. "But I'm coming back. I'll see you soon."

I clapped the phone shut, pacing with it in hand rather than pocketing it, even though I'd set the ringer at its highest volume, hoping she would call back before I was forced to turn it off. Roger was probably consoling her, she weepy in his arms, listening to my voice message again and calling me a goddamned liar. Kissing the salty tracks of tears, following them down to her lips.

We boarded, and as soon as I found my seat, I ordered a drink to quiet the conspiratorial voices in my head. The flight attendant refused to serve alcohol until we were in the air, so I fiddled with the air vent above me, adjusted the seat belt, lowered and raised the tray table, and flipped through the duty-free magazine, seeing but not seeing the pages as I turned them.

Checked my phone again.

Outside, a thick bank of mist rolled onto the runway, dressing the stage for another monsoon, darkening the cabin and transforming the safety glass window into a mirror.

Movement in the reflection, blue and white and red, and I was afraid to turn and look at the empty seat beside me because I had this oppressive sense, like chains attached from my soul to the floor, that I'd carried something bad to Phoenix with me, and now it was anxious to get back home.

"Excuse me, sir?" A flight attendant, her forehead lined with impatience, motioned to the empty seat. "I'm sorry to bother you, but the flight was overbooked. Are you traveling with a companion?"

If she only knew.

I shook my head, and the attendant made room for a little girl, blond hair braided in pigtails, all of eight or nine and with a voice so high and sweet it sounded like candy. She bounced into the seat, dutifully strapping her belt on and tightening it.

"*Bonjour,*" she said. "*Vous etes Français?*"

"American," I said, glancing at my phone one last time before powering it down. No calls. No surprise.

A thin, reedy woman wearing a comically large purple blouse sat across the aisle, reached over and tugged the girl's belt loop, shushing her.

The girl turned back to me and said, as slowly as if she were an adult speaking to a child, "*Je m'appelle Louise.*" She held a hand to her chest. "*Moi, Louise. Et vous?*"

I understood the girl, but I pretended not to. It was shaping up to be a long flight if someone didn't feed her some Ritalin.

"*Parlez-vous Français?*" she asked.

I shrugged.

"*Ouf.*" She slumped back, chin down, arms crossed. "*Pourquoi tout la monde ne parlent pas Français?*"

She wanted to know why the whole world didn't speak French. I wanted to know why she continued chattering at me for the duration of the flight, asking questions I couldn't answer, trying to teach me numbers and sounds, acting as my own personal translator when the men and women in uniform brought me beverage after beverage after beverage, even talking still after I stuffed a pair of headphones into my ears and flipped on the in-flight television embedded in the seat back in front of me.

The first program I came across was that old *Twilight Zone* episode. The one where some furry creature is on the wing of a plane, ripping out the engine's innards during a storm. It was the original, not the remade version with John Lithgow starring as the paranoid passenger, he being the only person to whom the creature showed itself. It seemed odd, not simply because several people on the show were smoking inside the airplane, but because of where *we* were, with a desert storm rolling in over us. I could think of but one worse program to watch on a flight.

And when I switched the channel, there it was. A documentary showing, on looped tape, multi-angle views of the 9/11 terrorist attacks.

Who screens this shit? I thought.

The cabin darkened as we flew into a wall of gray clouds, almost as dark as if we were flying at midnight.

I changed that channel as soon as I caught Louise, my annoying little friend, leaning over to see what I was watching, and settled on some crime show dubbed in French. I recognized the lead actor, that redheaded guy who always angles his head and speaks in grave tones, as if everything is as serious as murder. Even ordering a taco. I muted the sound and made up my own script.

"We're going down to the massage parlor later," the redheaded guy said, angling his head and speaking in grave tones. "If you want to come."

In the mean streets of Miami, they were. At least, that's what I thought. I'd never been to Miami. The redheaded cop was with another guy who smoked a cigar and wore sunglasses even though it was nighttime. They were lit up by a spotlight, a streetlamp that gave off far too much light to be anything other than artistic license.

"Nah," the other guy said, speaking my lines. "I gotta go to the laundromat. This guy stole my sheets." The cop nudged—practically kicked—a body that was draped over with white cloth, white cloth with spots of bright red here and there. "Made a real fuckin' mess of them, too."

Close-up on the redheaded guy, whose head angled further, so far his ear was almost on his shoulder. He slowly removed his own sunglasses. "What are those, four-hundred thread count Egyptian?"

I sipped at a vodka and coke I had mixed from one of those nip bottles, my eyelids starting to drop. The cigar-smoking guy on the show pulled out his dick and started to piss all over the shrouded corpse.

Louise wasn't looking, but I reflexively sat forward and tried to cover the screen while fumbling for the channel control. Again, I wondered, *Who runs this fucking network?*

The control was busted. None of the buttons worked anymore. I couldn't change the channel, couldn't turn it off, meanwhile the image on the screen now showed the shroud being peeled away from the corpse's head.

"No." I think I actually said it aloud because I felt Louise's attention—and not only Louise's, but others' as well—as I sat back. Sat back hard, like I was trying to push myself through the seat into the row behind me.

That little television screen, not much bigger than the cover of a paperback book, was grainy, but the dead face looked familiar, right down to the frozen, crooked grin and wire-thin John Lennon glasses.

"It can't be," I said, leaning forward to wipe a fingerprint of chocolate or potato chip grease from the screen.

The sound clicked back on so gradually that, at first, I thought the voice was in my head. "This is your fault," it said, an accent made even thicker by the sound of syrupy liquid bubbling up in his nose and mouth. "If you hadn't gone into the bar," it said, louder now through my headphones even though I had muted the sound, "if you hadn't started a fight, maybe Pierre would still be alive."

I blinked and saw—*thought* I saw—the dead man on the screen turn his head toward the camera, toward *me*, moving so slowly that I almost heard the joints in its neck creaking.

Pierre's voice roared out through its lips. "You did this to me."

I ripped the headphones out of my ears, yanked off my seat belt, and clambered over Louise, tripping over legs stretched out in the aisle, using the headrests I passed to hold myself up, heading down into the bathroom even though the seatbelt light was still on. I vomited my throat raw, tears burning through my sinuses. Kneeling over the toilet, telling myself it was all just a dream even though I had been wide awake, if a little tainted with alcohol, I vacuum flushed, stood on a pair of shaky legs, splashed cold water over my head.

A soft knock on the door brought me back around. A concerned flight attendant, most likely the one who'd had her eye on me for ordering so many drinks.

"Sir, are you alright?"

Was I?

I let her assist me back to my seat, leaning on her not so much for support but so she would think I was sick and not a *person of interest*. Her forearm felt warm under my clammy palm, warm and alive and real. When I sat, I noticed my television screen had changed. It now displayed a map of the world and a cartoonish airplane, plotting our route and showing where we were at that given moment. Somewhere over the Midwest.

I smiled at Louise, who no longer spoke but glanced at me cautiously, like I was the strangest person she'd ever met, and tried to sleep away my hallucination, afraid to stay awake yet terrified to dream.

But I did sleep, and I don't recall dreaming. As the plane began its descent into Paris, Louise shook me awake, apparently having decided I was just weird and not a danger, leaned over my lap and pointed to her arrondisement on the ground below. She and her mom lived in the eighteenth, she said, but her father lived in the twelfth. My ears popped and went dull, transforming the timbre of her speech into something far away and hollow.

We taxied to the gate, passengers already unbuckling and switching on mobile phones though the captain had advised otherwise. I turned on my own phone, watching a swell of jet fumes haze in the air outside, shimmering and rising from the engines. Engines that had not been torn apart by furry *Twilight Zone* creatures.

As soon as the phone powered up, it buzzed and vibrated in my palm. A single message, a text from Caroline. I caught my breath when I saw her name, relieved that she'd contacted me. Somewhere far deep in my psyche, somewhere I didn't want to go, I feared what she had to say.

Only six words, simple words that meant nothing separately, but awoke and stretched when put together. Six words that, according to the time stamp, she'd typed out eleven hours prior, right around the time my flight had departed from Phoenix.

Do not *come back to France,* the message read.

TEN

I ONCE READ AN article—*National Geographic,* I think it was, complete with the three-page foldout in the middle—describing Paris's underground, mapping it, measuring it larger and more elaborate than many modern-day cities. The subway was only part of it, and a small one at that, the touristic ossuary at One Place Denfert-Rochereau an even smaller part. Tangled beneath the city streets like yarn were thousands of tunnels and crumbling passageways, entries to those forbidden hallways usually hidden in dark alleys, sealed off with metal grates that the most curious always found a way around.

When I'd first come to Paris six months earlier with a group of American students, the catacombs were closed for repair. The Seine had been seeping into some of the passages, weakening the infrastructure in places and creating a potential flood hazard. I came back a few months later, on my own—incidentally, the same weekend I'd run into Pierre outside the opera house.

They had reopened the ossuary that day. Normally clogged with tourists of all races and nationalities, the place was empty save for myself and an English family on holiday. A mother and a father, and a daughter that could've been no more than Louise's age.

After buying a ticket and baby-stepping down a long flight of spiral stairs, the steps shorter in width than the length of my foot, cramped between stone walls that stank of mildew and dried earth, I came out into a series of rooms. Normal rooms with normal walls, and normal lights in the ceiling. Normal framed pictures of skulls and designs created out of human bones. I found it a relatively gentle way to prepare people, to soften the blow of what would come next.

Standing at the exit of the last room, a great archway that was bright on one side and dark on the other like the entryway of a haunted house, the English family had bottlenecked. The young girl stood at the threshold, arms splayed out, whimpering.

"I don't want to go in, Mommy. Pleasepleaseplease don't make me go in."

"This was your choice, honey," Mommy said, sounding as if she were trying very hard to keep her temper in check. "You said you wanted to come here for your birthday, so we're here."

"I changed my mind." With each word, the whimper grew more desperate, more terrified, and eventually degraded into sobs of panic. "Don't make me go," she said.

"There's nothing to be afraid of," Mommy said. "This is how we all end up someday."

Maybe Mommy was genuine in her attempt to calm the girl, but her choice of words immediately struck her from the Mother Of The Year nomination list.

The parents dragged their daughter inside, and my heart ached for that little girl. But she fought the terror, clamping her lips shut and only making the smallest of squeaks at some of the more gruesome displays.

Happy birthday, I thought.

Home to some six million people, the stone mines underground claimed their bodies after the war, when the city boasted more corpses than Catholic cemeteries had room for. In typical Parisian fashion, the ossuary became art, bones delicately placed in piles and lined along the walls. A hallway of femurs here, a hallway of humeri there. Skulls accented this checkerboard of remains, peering out from a number of different geometric patterns. In one wall, the skulls formed the shape of a heart, a morbid reference to the romance of Paris, that eternal city of lovers. Lights burned much lower in this portion of the catacombs, setting the proper atmosphere, and no flash photography—no photography at all, for that matter—was allowed.

The English mother's words came back to me. *This is how we all end up someday.*

There was something beautiful and desolate in this eerie silence, more sorrowful than scary. I reached out and placed my fingertips inches away from a cracked skull, wondering who this person had been, what he or she had done with life. Had any of them, at any time, stopped to consider—as I was thinking of it then—how tragic, how depressing it would be to face death knowing they'd simply be tossed underground with millions of other corpses, and put on display like some biological art exhibit?

I felt no ghosts in there though, and I wondered if the birthday girl had felt the same, since I no longer heard her struggling to control her breaths. I paused for a moment and held my own, looking around, realizing it had been some time since I'd heard the family's footsteps and whispered observations. They had either moved far ahead of me or dropped far behind. I was alone.

Alone with several million dead people, of course.

And though I had entered the ossuary as a tourist, curious and worry free, I suddenly felt like an inhabitant, like someone who belonged there, when I noticed I was alone. A completely irrational sensation, I know, but the rules change when you're in a situation like that. It's like lying in bed at night, reading a creepy novel by low light, and you catch a glimpse of something white and formless rushing past your door in the dark of the hallway beyond. Your heart starts to pound and you bite back a scream, knowing there's nothing out there, but . . . *what if there is?* You hold the book a little higher, blocking the doorway out of your vision because if it remains in your sight, even in the periphery, you'll keep looking, and if you keep looking you're certain you *will* see something out there, and you won't be able to move when it comes for you.

It was quiet, but not totally; from somewhere in those tunnels came the slow drip of moisture from the ceilings.

I started walking in the direction of the exit, sweating even in the cool air, somewhere between a walk and a jog. I'd never been claustrophobic, but considering the number of mental afflictions plaguing my mother, I entertained the possibility of it running in the family. I moved from the macabre ossuary into a tunnel so thin I couldn't stretch my arms out completely, a ceiling so low I almost felt it brushing against my hair.

I fought the urge to run. To run, in my current state, was to admit—even subconsciously—that there was something to run *from*. And if there was something to run from, I was sure my heart would just pop like an overfilled water balloon.

And now, a half day after leaving Phoenix, I found myself again at Charles de Gaulle airport, standing at the top of an escalator, remembering the claustrophobia in the catacombs as I'd descended into the underground graveyard. I felt torn in two, like part of me was moving backward.

Halfway down I closed my eyes, unable to watch the travelers' warped reflections in the metal siding, unable to look down without dropping into vertigo. I tasted bile and dry airplane chicken in the back of my throat. When the escalator leveled off, it spit us out onto a platform where we rounded a corner, and then mobbed onto another escalator. We sank into the depths of the airport like cattle being led into a basement slaughterhouse, heading for the train that would take us into the city proper—the same ride I'd taken almost a week ago, but in reverse—and where another train would depart for Pau in less than an hour.

At Gare de L'est, I was directed to a sleeper—an overnight

car—with two other men. Both wore suits and carried small travel bags that implied they were in the city either on business or to visit mistresses. Beds were stacked three high on either side of a walkway almost thin enough to require sideways shuffling. The two men chose the top bunks, the first falling asleep almost immediately and snoring in such a fashion that his lips flapped together when he exhaled. The other cranked his iPod so high that I could hear Lady Gaga or Beyoncé or some bouncy dance shit pulsing through his earphones. I crawled into the lowest bunk, stuffed a pair of foam plugs into my ears. They muffled but failed to kill the snoring, the music, the ring and rattle and clang of iron wheels speeding across iron tracks. The very same tracks, I remembered, that brought French Jews to the death camps during World War II.

Sometime around six in the morning, just as the sun appeared from behind a steeple of mountains, I grabbed my pack and moved out to the hallway when one of my roommates began thrashing around in his sleep, moaning like a man possessed.

The hills gradually colored from black to brown to green as the sun rose, the surroundings changing from sparse farmland to suburbia to the outskirts of urban sprawl. We screeched to a halt in front of a faded blue sign that read PAU, sleepy-eyed commuters on the landing platform grabbing their bags and heading toward the train's doors.

I took three steps down onto the pavement, inhaling doughy scents of fresh warm bread and the earthy moisture of mountain streams close by. For better or worse, I was back where I needed to be.

At the top of Rue Serviez, just as I crossed the road that would take me to my shower and my bed, two desperately needed luxuries after more than twenty-four hours of travel, a familiar voice called out from a side street. From the direction of Le Garage, a mostly English pub on the east side of town.

"Jerry," he said. The accent was thick and slurred, Australian and drunk. "What the fuck, mate?"

Roger Watford wobbled toward me, stepping over a curb and tripping on the toe of his sandal, nearly face planting in the process.

Would I have caught him if he'd fallen?

"I thought you went home, man," he said, clasping my shoulder, breath toxic in my face.

He noticed my frown, raised his eyebrows as a silent question. Only Caroline knew I'd gone home to see my father.

"It's not even seven o'clock," I said, "and you're already plastered."

He pointed a finger to the sky. "*Still* plastered, you mean. From last night."

Roger and I had only hung out a handful of times, usually as parts of separate groups with mutual members. Caroline was most often at the center of the circle which connected us. Roger was jovial enough after the first few hoists, always willing to buy a round for anyone standing nearby. But, a bit like my father, after a certain number of drinks, the light in Roger's eyes switched off and he became the type to break things for no reason.

"Come have a drink with me," he said, leaning so close that his sweaty forehead rubbed against mine.

"I have to talk to Caroline."

"Just a shot. It'll be quick." Then his expression changed, closed off and guarded now as if what I'd just said had taken a few seconds to register. "Caroline?"

"Is she at home?" I mentally swiped away an image of them brushing their teeth together at the same bathroom sink, trying not to unfairly condemn Roger.

His fingers tightened on my shoulder. "What do you want to talk to her about?"

"It's between us," I said, gently shrugging off his hand and sliding backward a step.

"Haven't you heard?"

"I've been gone," I reminded him. "I haven't heard anything."

"First," he said, holding up two fingers, "her brother was killed."

I gave nothing of my thoughts away, unaware of how much he knew about that night.

"Second, Caroline was supposed to meet some chink for a tutor sesh the other day, but she never showed."

"Caroline or the—" I paused. Swallowed the slur. "The Chinese student?"

"Caroline."

"When?"

"Day before yesterday. Nobody's seen her since."

She'd sent her last message, warning me not to come back, yesterday morning, but I didn't tell Roger that. Was she trying to protect *me* with that message? Or protect herself?

Could it be as simple—but as heartbreaking—as she just didn't want me around?

"What about her stuff?" I asked. "Maybe she took off for a while. Needed to get away."

Roger shook his head. "Clothes, jewelry, everything's still at the flat."

She's probably with family, I thought. But for all I knew, Pierre was the only family she had.

"I'm not sure I heard the whole story," I said. "What happened to Pierre?"

Roger's pupils darkened, two black holes growing in his face, and I sensed that Caroline had told him I was with her brother that night. "What do you care?"

"He was my teacher," I said. "And Caroline's brother. Jesus, isn't that enough?"

Roger lowered his hands and recoiled as if I'd hit him.

"What?" I moved back another step, just out of kicking

distance.

"You saying I don't care?"

"Of course not. Did I say that?"

"It sure sounded like it."

"Roger," I said, holding my palms up. "You're overreacting. I know you care."

"I do."

"I know."

"I'm not a heartless fuck."

"I know that."

"But you said it like I *wanted* the guy to get hurt or something."

"Roger, you're imagining things."

"*They* talked to me like that, too."

"Who?"

"The fucking cops, mate. Who else?" Roger shivered like the adrenaline of combat was beginning to drip into his system. Considering the amount of alcohol that must've been in his blood, the drip could become a flood in a matter of seconds.

Didn't I know it.

It hit me then that I was like a magnet for violence. Was there a pull, something that drew me toward potentially aggressive situations? Or was there something *in me* that drew this type of behavior out of others? Had I spent all those years training, all those years treating the symptoms of my anger and not the root?

"Roger," I said, "I know you didn't have anything to do with it. I was with him that night."

A sudden twist of his lips made me instantly regret I'd said that. She hadn't told him.

"You were with him?" he asked.

"I walked home with him. Watched him go inside and heard the door latch."

"What were *you* doing with him?"

"We went over some sociology notes for class." More

truth than lie, though not entirely accurate.

I could almost hear the gears turning inside his head. He ruffled a hand through sandy, brittle hair, and smiled. The gesture was so calculated, so fake, that I expected him to wink at me.

"Why don't you go home," I said, changing tack in an effort to derail whatever nefarious thoughts were bouncing around in there. The smile alone unnerved me. "You're tanked."

"Yeah," he said, grin widening, but no longer meeting my gaze. "But come have a drink with me tonight?"

It was a bad idea, I knew. And I don't know why I did it, but I agreed to meet him at Galway. Possibly just to get him away from me now. Each moment that passed here made the air a little thicker.

"Eight o'clock," he said.

"Sleep it off, Roger."

He turned and walked off, his step noticeably steadier than it had been five minutes prior. I kept my eyes on him until he disappeared from view, thinking that—drunk or not—Roger certainly didn't appear too concerned about the whereabouts of his vanished roommate.

On my cell phone, reading that final message again—Do *not* come back—I pressed reply, and typed two words.

"Why not?"

The text bounced back as undeliverable.

ELEVEN

I DROPPED MY BAGS at the dorm, showered up but resisted the urge to fall into bed, instead aiming straight for the campus and the faculté des lettres to see if Malcolm McCormack, the study abroad director, had heard about Caroline. Something about Roger's story made me uneasy, but my overtired brain couldn't pinpoint what it was. Something more than just his nonchalant reaction, I was sure.

I crossed the lawn, a long stretch of green the length of a soccer field, steam rising off of the grass. Most of the students and staff were on summer vacation. The few faces I saw were unfamiliar, and wearing masks of cautious good humor. They'd recently lost a teacher, a co-worker, maybe a friend. Laughter was gentle and self-consciously halted, as if it were too soon to be anything but quiet and respectful. To do anything but mourn.

I found Malcolm in the faculté foyer, dropping coins into a coffee dispenser. Unhealthily thin for his six-foot-six inch frame, bony fingers tentatively poking buttons, Malcolm glanced down at me and then back at the keypad as if I were a stranger.

For one brief second, Malcolm's image in the coffee machine's glass front was wrong. It was rounder, fatter, lips swollen and cheek split open, exposing bone, transposed over a photo of a smartly manicured hand gripping a mug, heat coming from the cup in waves. Malcolm's arm passed in front of the machine and then Pierre was gone, replaced by the emaciated, sunken-cheeked face of my study abroad advisor.

"Did you see that?" I said, twisting my hands together. "Please tell me you saw that."

I'm not sure why I said it. Not sure why I hoped Malcolm had seen it. I suppose it'd be easier to accept that we'd both seen a ghost or both noticed a trick of the light, rather than admit I was losing my mind.

"Saw what?"

A small, plastic cup dropped from inside the bowels of the machine, and the liquid that poured out stank of rust or copper. Under the pale, fluorescent rail lighting in the ceiling, the coffee came out looking red.

"Malcolm," I said, stepping back, unsteady, feeling like I was walking a tightrope between a dream and reality.

"Jarrod," he said, turning at the mention of his name, awake now and recognizing me. "I thought you went home."

"Word gets around pretty fast here." I looked at his reflection, at the stream of liquid pissing into a cup. The reflection was Malcolm's. The liquid was black. Smelled like coffee, albeit thin, watery vending machine variety.

Not stale blood, at least.

"Are you okay?" he asked.

"I'm wondering the same thing about you."

He shrugged. "I'm glad you're back." There was no conviction in his words. They were as lifeless as a flatline.

"I heard about Pierre."

Malcolm was quiet for a long time, unmoving, even once his coffee had finished dispensing. "Kind of hard not to," he finally said.

When he faced me, stepping forward into a space better lit, it might have been him who was the ghost. He was originally from Ohio, I thought, with the pasty complexion of a midwestern computer nerd who'd been home schooled to avoid bullying by the hard drinking defensive linemen on the football team. But, somehow, it was possible for him to appear even more pale than usual. Purple bags hung like quarter moons under his eyes, and his lips cracked at the corners.

He looked back at his coffee, seemed no longer interested in it and left it there, starting toward his office. "Walk with me," he said.

Every inch of wall space in Malcolm's office was covered with posters, postcards, luscious greenery scenes and colorful garden shots of Pau in summer, photographs of smiling students in ridiculous poses in front of famous European monuments. Tour de France cyclists pedaling through the streets of downtown. Beside his cluttered desk sat a table with neat piles of brochures; everything from maps to safe sex guides, and even a bowl of condoms individually wrapped like collegiate candy.

And just to the right of his desk, Malcolm's only personal item. A poster of Jimmy Page standing within a cloud of smoke, onstage, slinging a violin bow across the strings of his Les Paul.

I shut the door behind us.

"What can I do for you, Jarrod?" Malcolm lowered himself into his chair, a man well aged years before his time. And his time, I guessed, couldn't have been much older than my own.

"Is there something I can do for *you?*"

He waved my offer away, lazily swatting the air as if a mosquito buzzed around him. "I'm simply in stage four of loss. Depression. Acceptance is next, but good God if it won't come quickly."

"You guys were close." A statement, not a question, though I didn't really know.

"Pierre was the first teacher who really accepted me. To everyone else, I was just another American trying to plant my flag in French soil. We used to go out, the four of us."

"The four of you?"

"My wife and I. And Pierre and his wife, Audrey."

I'd forgotten Pierre had a wife, and hearing her name snapped a blurry picture back into focus.

"She's a mess, Jarrod. You think I look bad? You should see her."

In uncomfortable situations, people tend to look at their hands. I looked down at mine, inspecting the knuckles and turning them over, tracing the lines on my palms, embarrassed now that Malcolm had begun to cry. I didn't want to feel like a voyeur.

"And the kid," he said.

At that, I raised my head.

"Man, that poor kid." Malcolm leaned forward, rapping his head against the desktop.

"Pierre has—" The rest of the question got stuck behind my teeth.

Malcolm didn't lift his head, just rolled it back and forth. "Not yet. Audrey's about four months out."

That made it worse. I couldn't help but think of Jeanette back home, wondering if she was four months out, too.

In one swift motion, Malcolm sat up and stretched, sucking in oxygen and wiping the tears away with his sleeve. "Anyway," he said, "life goes on."

"For some of us," I said, inspecting my hands again. Trying to read my fortune. I'd felt guilty for not protecting Pierre. But now? Now there was a child involved, a child that would never know its father.

Guilt doesn't even begin to describe it.

"Have the police spoken with you yet?"

"The police?" I asked. I shouldn't have been surprised. By now, Caroline would certainly have told them I'd been with her brother that night.

"Routine questioning, they said. But word is they found Pierre's wallet in a trashcan here on campus. They've been interviewing all the students, faculty, janitors. Everybody." He pulled a collection of business cards from his pocket, dropped half of them, cursed, and rifled through the rest until finding the one he sought. "The inspector's number," he said, holding the card out. "You should probably call him before he comes looking for you."

"What about Caroline?" I asked. "What happened to her?"

"What do you mean?" Malcolm said.

"I heard she went missing."

"Did you tell the police that?"

"I just got back, Malcolm. This morning. I haven't spoken to anyone."

"Well," he said, "I'm sure they'll catch you eventually."

His choice of words gave me a start.

"Catch up to you, I mean."

TWELVE

I PASSED OUT IN my room, too confused and concerned and worried to think straight, waking in a haze sometime around seven-thirty that night, thinking at first that I was still in Arizona, my heart beating so hard that it shook the bed on its weak, skeletal frame. An awful dream still held its claws in my memory before fading, like a screaming child with hands wrapped tightly around a pair of monkey bars. I couldn't recall details, only a sensation of pure, breathless terror, and that I'd realized I was dreaming and tried to wake myself up by yelling, but the noise that came out was nothing more than a dead wheeze.

I scratched dried gum from my eyes, switched on the bedside lamp, and saw my luggage—still packed—at the foot of the bed. A tiny table pushed up against the wall. An even tinier kitchen area with only two stovetop burners and a sink so small it would only hold a day's worth of dirty dishes.

All real, all tangible. At that point, it was Arizona that seemed like a dream.

She had snuck into the classroom without anyone really noticing. Pierre scribbled some notes on the whiteboard, things for us to concentrate on. We had two weeks to study for our first exam. Reading comprehension, writing, conversation. All rooted in sociology, the study of people and their habits, their behaviors. He wrote this in French, though most of us were totally green, because he believed immersion was the best way to learn about anything.

"If you need any help studying," I believe he'd said, and focusing on me when he did, "Mademoiselle Fontaine will assist you."

The class turned its collective head, and Caroline's cheeks went the color of burning embers. She blew a raspberry at Pierre, who grinned in return.

By the end of class, she'd commanded my complete attention. She'd sat there taking notes, watching a couple of bluebirds chasing each other around outside, correcting the two Russian students nearest to her. I'd noticed the way she crossed her feet when she leaned forward. The way she fingered her hoop earring with her left hand while she wrote with her right. The way her chin bunched up in lines when she laughed.

At the bell, while the other students lingered and practiced their French rather than lapsing with relief into their native languages, I rolled my notebook into my back pocket, wove my way through the class, and ran into Pierre on my way out.

"*J'espère que tu vas utiliser la Mademoiselle a votre avantage*," I thought he said. Much later, after I'd completely fallen for her and earned Pierre's scorn, I found it funny, that line. Hoping that I'd use Caroline to my advantage.

I'd run into her at the Cap Sud café later that afternoon. She recognized me from class and as natural as taking a breath, leaned in for the cheek-to-cheek kiss.

"*Salut*," she said, stirring my insides as her skin brushed against mine.

"*Ça va?*" I asked.

She said she was doing well. Spoke slowly, simply enough for me to understand.

"Are you ready for your test?" she asked.

"I've never been good at tests."

"I am practicing to be a teacher," she said. "Like Monsieur Coudreau. I could help you study. It will help me, too."

And then I met Roger Watford who, in seeing Caroline, greeted her in perfect French and perfect kiss. Her speech sped up when they talked, and all traces of Roger's Aussie accent disappeared.

"You coming to the boulevard tonight?" he asked, clamping down on my shoulder as if we'd known each other for years.

"He can't go," Caroline said. "I'm helping him study."

"You can study at Galway. What better place to talk to real French people?" *Real*, like the people I met in supermarkets and restaurants were a somehow inferior breed.

Caroline said something—I couldn't tell where one word left off and the next began—and they both started laughing. Then she turned to me and said, "Looks like we are studying at Galway tonight."

And there I was again, meeting Roger instead of Caroline this time, and he was already at Galway when I arrived, sitting alone and nursing a beer. A couple of guys pushed the bar's slide away doors open, a steady stream of patrons moving from the dark sofas inside to the busy patio where Bordeaux had just kicked off against Nice on huge flat screen televisions mounted under the overhang.

Roger wasn't watching. He wasn't even facing the bar, but staring out into the darkness on the other side of the boulevard and the spotty lights of the train station below.

I ordered a Guinness, pulled up a chair beside him, and asked, "How're you feeling?" I didn't like Roger, but I guess I didn't hate him, either. At least, not then.

"Head hurts."

"That hair of the dog shit never works."

He chuckled. "Dog shit."

"You sleep at all?" I asked. Roger wore different clothes than I'd seen him in that morning, but smelled like cheese left out to rot in the sun.

"I saw something on the news," he said. "They might have a lead on Pierre's killer."

Again, his casual manner, as if he were reciting soccer scores from a bunch of B-league matches, made me uneasy. And something about that word *killer* set me on edge, too. It was somehow harsher, more vulgar than *murderer*.

"Think it might be one of the students." Roger sucked loudly at the foam on his beer.

I knew that wasn't right. Chances were much greater that one of the guys from the nameless bar—most likely that skinhead character—followed us to Pierre's after the fight, maybe *expecting* Pierre to come back out for his notebook.

"Why else," Roger said, "would someone murder him outside of his own apartment, then dump his wallet and glasses in a campus trashcan? They're kilometers apart."

"It doesn't make sense," I said. "The wallet, okay. Someone robbed him and dumped the evidence far away from the scene. But his glasses? Why take them?"

Roger's eyes met mine, and it seemed we shared the same idea. But he quickly looked away, as if he'd been caught sharing something he shouldn't have shared.

That same sensation from earlier in the day, when Roger and I had first spoken, washed over me. Sort of an otherworldly, ethereal warning, like ESP or a sixth sense, like Roger was sending out unconscious signals of intent and I just happened to be picking them up. A bad liar will look up when he lies, but a practiced one will look you in the eye without faltering. Both are telling. Roger pretended not to have known that I'd spent that last night with Pierre, but *of course* Caroline had already told him. She shared everything else with him. Why would she hide that?

And the glasses. Malcolm hadn't said anything about Pierre's glasses, neither had the news reports, only that his wallet was found in a trashcan on campus. But when I mentioned them just then, Roger had flinched. Almost imperceptibly, but he'd flinched as if he knew he'd slipped up.

I saw it, now, as clear as polished glass, in his every movement. The way he shifted his gaze when I stared right into his eyes. The way he looked through the bottom of his pint when he drank.

He was trying to set me up.

A passerby bumped into my chair and I turned on instinct. Nothing more sinister than an intoxicated Bordeaux fan, waving in sincere apology and continuing on his way. But when I looked back at Roger, I thought I saw a pair of hands cupped around his ear, and a disembodied face above them, before they too vanished into the crowd.

Or vanished into my mind.

Something in Roger had changed. His shifty, uncertain movements became steady, confident, the red rings around his eyes dulling and smoothing out.

"Caroline and I dated a bit," he said. "Before she met you."

"Is that so." I frowned, not liking this sudden turn in the conversation.

"We went out a couple of times. She wasn't too interested."

"Imagine that."

"Her brother was already—" He cocked his head again, as if listening closely to someone else's whispered words. "—he was already getting into crazy shit. She was worried about him."

I clenched my pint glass, if only to keep my hand from shaking. He was laying out verbal traps, little pits for me to fall into. Testing my patience, trying to wind me up.

And it was working.

"She told me to make friends with him," he said. "But Pierre was having none of it." He laughed. *Laughed.* "You know what I'm talking about."

"Do I?" I said, dialing up every ounce of self-control to

not put my fist through his teeth.

"After he died—after you left—"

Roger laid a particular emphasis on my leaving, enough to sound as if he were accusing me of something.

"Caroline was wrecked," he continued. "Naturally. We went drinking one night, drowning the sorrows and all that. Had a good time, but . . ." He stared off into the distance. "I think I pushed her too far."

I set my glass down, curled my fists beneath the table. "Her brother was killed," I said. "Do you get that? Does that affect you at all?"

"I didn't mean to take advantage," he said, maybe registering my comment, maybe not. "I wasn't, like, preying on her emotional vulnerability or anything."

"What did you do?" I asked, slowly, separating the syllables as if each was its own sentence. It wasn't jealousy causing me to react the way I did. It was the thought of Roger hurting Caroline in her moment of weakness. A moment I would have been there to protect her from, had I not been called back to Arizona.

"We were in an alley by Le Garage," he said. "I don't even remember how we got there, only bits and pieces. I pushed her up against a wall and kissed her. I didn't think it was a big deal—we'd made out before." Roger said this last bit with a smile, an instigating glimmer in his eye.

"Where did she go, Roger?" I said, refusing to let him bait me. "She didn't disappear, did she? She fucking left."

"She tried to shove me away," he said, not hearing me at all. Completely wrapped up in his story. "I couldn't control myself."

"Did she leave because of me?" I asked. "Or did she leave because of you?"

"I just touched her, that's all. But it wasn't right. I know it wasn't right."

"Have a drink on me, asshole." I pushed my beer toward him, knocking it into his and sending both glasses into his lap.

I felt myself slipping. If I stayed, I might have fallen into that uncontrollable fury I'd experienced in the schoolyard that day, when I'd beaten Josh Thompson for tripping me, but continued beating him because I'd imagined my father's face superimposed over his.

I walked to the end of the boulevard as calmly as I could, feeling Roger's eyes on me. When I reached a corner I cut it sharp, and then, once out of that little fucker's sight, starting running at full clip to burn off the desire to turn around and do something I'd regret.

THIRTEEN

AS MUCH AS I'D pursued her the last few months, Caroline always managed to pull me close with one hand and keep me at arm's length with the other. Like she viewed our relationship—or our *interpersonal transactions*, as she sometimes called them—as some illicit affair. When we were seen in public, it had to appear platonic. Two study partners. Nothing more. She didn't want her brother to know.

I wondered then if she didn't want Roger to know.

But the whole thing was a confusing mess because there hadn't really been anything to hide.

In keeping with our clandestine flirtations, her apartment was off limits. She insisted on privacy. I'd agreed, deflected, pretended to understand. Refused to openly admit that it made me sick to even think of running into Roger there.

Now I stood outside stabbing her doorbell, something I'd never done before, convinced Caroline had not *vanished* or *disappeared* at all. Convinced Roger had been stringing me along this whole time.

A pair of six-foot high, milky glass panes framed the door on either side. I cupped my hands and peered inside, but saw only clouded and blurry shapes, furniture on the floor and framed images on the walls. I took out my cell phone, dialed Caroline's number, and pressed my ear to the glass, listening for a ring in the apartment. But it didn't ring, not in the apartment and not in my ear. It went straight to voicemail, so I tried to text her again but received that same old message:

indisponible. Undeliverable.

A couple of teenagers, a girl and a boy as far as I could tell, but mildly androgynous—I suppose they could have both been girls or both been boys—rounded the block. Interlaced fingers tipped with black nail polish. They might have even been twins, I thought, with too white flesh and too small t-shirts stretched like taut black skin, until they attempted to tie their tongue rings together. They stopped at a door on the opposite side of the street, one of them fishing a key from an impossibly tight pair of jeans.

"Hey," I said. "Do you know the people who live here?"

"*Pardon?*" They said in unison.

I pointed at the door. "Caroline Fontaine?"

They exchanged a glance, eyebrows scrunched.

"Roger Watford?" I said.

The couple turned away, shrugging. Whispering. Entering quickly into their own building before shutting themselves in. Locks slid into place, followed by the dull rattle of a door chain. There were no such thing as friendly neighbors on this side of town.

A second story window in Caroline's apartment yawned open, it being the only access to a wrought iron balcony attached to the wall below. It was a fire escape, maybe, but useless without a ladder or other scalable apparatus attached. The gray stonewalls beneath and all around were smoothed by rain, almost sanded to a polish. A tempting entrance, that window, but nothing more than temptation with no way to reach it.

I banged on the glass one last time, knowing it was futile. If Caroline wasn't gone, she was inside and hiding from something. Maybe even me.

No, I thought. *She's not hiding. She's grieving.*

"She doesn't want to see me," I said aloud, reluctantly accepting. I jogged home, heading north up Rue Carnot, then hooking a left at Alsace Lorraine by Domino's pizza and a Subway sandwich shop. American cultural invasion at its finest. "She doesn't want to see *anyone*," I said, huffing between breaths, drawing suspicious stares from dog walkers and school children. "Understandable. Christ, her brother just died."

I cut another right, toward the campus and the dorms and ran up Rue Des Frères Wright, the street where the Wright Brothers lived, for a time, while designing the world's first operational aircraft. I ran past bus stops with schedules and advertisements, George Clooney smirking as he held up a glass of coffee. Charlize Theron dressed in sparkles that barely covered her naughtiest bits, emblazoned over with the tag *J'adore Dior*. A man and a woman, he in black tux, she in billowing white dress, standing before a priest in some Parisian church.

Caroline once told me it was her childhood dream to have a wedding in Paris, which is peculiar, because Jeanette had said something similar. She—Jeanette, not Caroline—thought it was the most sensual city in the world. Now that I think about it, Caroline had used that same word. Sensual.

And I suppose, if you put a picture of Jeanette alongside one of Caroline, they shared features I've always been drawn to. High, crabapple cheekbones. Almond shaped eyes. A smattering of freckles across their noses. Behaviorally, one was like a photo negative of the other. Jeanette, quiet and reserved and maybe lacking a bit of self-confidence. Caroline, vibrant and brash with a confidence level that bordered on arrogant.

Put the two together and you had my dream girl.

Outside the dorms, dripping with cooled sweat, I let myself in the building and—for once—forewent the stairs and chose the elevator. I pressed the button for my floor, absently reading over declarations scratched into the metal casing by foreign students and locals alike.

Brandi and Jacob forever!

and

Fuck capitalism!

and
Vas te faire foutre!
and
Free Bertrand Cantat!
and
Your mother sucks cock!

The elevator doors opened and a flock of youngish girls came romping down the hallway, motion lights flicking on in time with the song they were dancing to. Some horrible, poppy tune that had taken the continent by storm. Tokio Hotel, I thought it was, a group of musicians who couldn't decide if they wanted to be women or men.

One of the girls broke off from her friends, stopping me as I stuck my key into the lock of room 402.

"You're Jarrod Nelson?" she said, no accent to speak of. She might have even been part of my study abroad group. There were far too many of these girls to keep track of and they all looked alike, wearing black tights and bright miniskirts, just like all their French counterparts.

"Somebody was looking for you earlier," she said, the stud in her lip bobbing up and down as she spoke. "Banged on your door for, like, a fuckin' hour."

"A whole hour?" I asked, smiling a little so she would think I was joking and not just annoyed.

Her friends had gathered at the elevator door, talking low in French with butchered accents. "Come *on*, Renata," one of them said, pressing the call button again and again.

"Yeah," Renata said, nodding with intent, my sarcasm completely lost on her. "He asked if I knew you—he was sketchy, like a fucking skaz or something, but in a suit and tie and jacket and stuff—and I said I didn't know you from Adam. My mom used to say that all time, *I don't know you from Adam.* I guess it fits 'cause I have no fucking idea who Adam is, but—"

"Thank you," I said, unlocking my door and stepping inside.

Renata's friends broke up in laughter, and as I shut the door behind me, she cursed back, saying, "You guys are jerks."

I switched on the light, leaned back on the door and let out a long, slow breath. Who the hell wanted to see me so badly that they'd knock on my door for, like, a fuckin' hour? Probably not Malcolm. Those girls were American, and if indeed from my group, they would have known Malcolm from Adam. And it couldn't have been Roger. I was with him at the time.

I dug through my pockets, found a single, crumpled euro bill slightly dampened with sweat, drink receipts with that same flimsy quality, change, and the business card Malcolm had given me. *Inspecteur Stephan Gerardy*, it read, with a phone number, and a downtown address listed.

"You should probably call him before he comes looking for you," I heard Malcolm say.

"They think it was one of the students," I heard Roger say.

I had done nothing wrong. Like Malcolm had said, it was just routine questioning. Still, it was difficult for me to swallow, like I had a golf ball lodged in my throat, when I thought about this faceless Gerardy character at my door while I was away. Surely Caroline had told him I was with Pierre by now. And Roger probably had, too.

My laundry was still hanging from a string that led from the door to the oval-shaped window facing opposite, socks and shirts and underwear dangling from hangers attached to small hooks in the ceiling. I pulled everything down, methodically, folding each item in a way I had never done back home. Something—maybe a growing seed of anxiety, maybe the idea that I could keep my mind controlled by keeping my body busy—compelled me to clean up, to sweep and mop the floors and scrub the toilet and shower (there was still some blood from my head injury streaked around the edge of the drain) so furiously that my hands were sore afterward. Then I sat at my laptop, wrinkled fingertips poised over the keys, not really sure what I was looking for.

Out of habit, I checked my email. There was already a message from my mother.

FOURTEEN

DEAR J,

I'VE TRIED several times to call the number you gave me, but the telephone makes funny noises whenever I dial. I talked to the operator once, and she was about as helpful as that Arab woman at the supermarket downtown. Dial one, then the country code, then one again, then the number, she said, or something like that, but I think she forgot to add that I'm supposed to throw my hands in the air and twirl like a cheerleader, click my heels together three times, and then wish on a falling star. I've called the number before, I told her. She tried to patch me through, but she put me through to 9-1-1. Can you believe that? They sent a police officer to check on me. Sweet boy. Very nice of him. Anyway, I'm emailing you because I think your phone has been disconnected. That worries me, Jarrod. You should have a phone.

You haven't been gone long, and things have already gone crazy here. I think you took all the normalcy with you, and I wish you'd bring it back.

First, your father had another accident. He was working in the shop, trying to hammer something, but the hammer— he said—wouldn't line up with the metal. (I think it was probably his eyes that wouldn't line up.) I heard him from inside the house, cursing up a storm, banging and banging and banging.

Anyhoo—is that what you kids say these days? Anyhoo?—

he swung the hammer down one too many times and it slipped right through his fingers and smashed three of his toes. We've always had long toes, Jarrod, me and your father and you too, of course. It's a wonder they don't get hurt more often.

My God, that man can wail when he wants to (which isn't often, as you know . . . that would be a sign of weakness, wouldn't it? And we just couldn't have that), but please don't ask why he was in the garage alone. And please don't ask why he was barefoot. I feel bad enough about letting him wander away. I don't need your judgment. Okay?

Lord, I ran so fast I almost tripped and broke my leg on that awful stump between the house and the garage. You really have to do something about that, you know, when you get back. I've asked your father a thousand times, but, well, he sure as a bag of frozen horse patties won't be able to do it now.

There was black smoke pouring out of the workshop door when I finally got there—limping like a cripple in my own right. My best guess is that your father lost his balance when he threw the hammer, bumped into the forge (which was lit, Jesus be with us), and spilled hot coals all over the floor. He says he doesn't know what happened. I pulled him aside before the fire had grown too badly out of control. A few small burns on his arms, first degree on his face, and all his hair was singed off. Eyebrows too, even. He's in the ICU recovering. I've just returned home. They took the bandages off today. He looks like the love child of Mr. Clean and that Nightmare on Elm Street guy.

I'm sorry for joking. It's not funny, really, but Jarrod, I swear, if I don't laugh right now I'm going to cry. And if I cry, I might not stop crying. I know there's something IMPORTANT you have to take care of out there, but we— your family, you know, those who raised you and loved you since before you were born?—are important too. Please consider coming home. For good. Please? I'm not sure I can do this alone.

Second. Jeanette stopped by. She looks a little plump, Jarrod, and if I know anything about women (and I like to think I do, considering I've been one my whole life), I'd bet your father's insurance policy that she's pregnant. I'd bet four or five months pregnant, my watch on it. Six, on the high end.

GET A PHONE. If you need money, tell me.

Love,

Mom.

P.S. When was the last time you and Jeanette were "together"?

FIFTEEN

YOU TOOK ALL THE normalcy with you, she'd written. I
don't know what world she lived in, but life there was never
normal. And in fact, during that short period I was home, it
was even *less* normal than usual.

I took a cold shower—it was Saturday, the building
owners always shut off the hot water on the weekends. I
pictured my dad laid up in a hospital bed, mummified with
wraps to cover the burn scars, and as much as I may have
hated him at times, I worried for him. My mother couldn't
take care of him. She used to say he'd be the death of her,
but the way things were going, it might end up the other way
around. She wanted me to come home—and a very small
part of me wanted to as well, if only to escape my
responsibility here—but what would that solve? I would
become Dad's caregiver, at least until he crushed my head
with a hammer while I slept or took the skin from my face
with a pair of metal shears. And if I *did* take care of him,
would I feel like I had made up for my inability to protect
Pierre? Like I had redeemed myself, at least in my own
eyes?

I doubted it. Pierre would always be with me if I ran away.
That was all Caroline had asked. *Protect my brother.*
And Mom's postscript shook me up too, assigning words
to an idea I had of course considered, but didn't want to
accept. Jeanette and I, we'd had Going Away Sex right
before I'd left for France. Our behaviors were modified by

emotion, and more than a little alcohol, that night. I couldn't recall whether or not we'd used any kind of protection.

Stupid, I thought. *Stupid, stupid, stupid.*

I didn't bother to dress after my shower, instead climbing right into bed. A vision of Caroline, our final meeting at an Italian restaurant downtown, formed behind my eyelids. Her hair was up at first, exposing a long and slim white neck and a tiny dark mole just underneath her left ear. Then the hair was down, lazy curls brushing against the curve of her shoulders like waves lapping at a deserted beach. But I couldn't see her face, its features shimmering, transforming. Then she was Jeanette, strawberry blonde hair tied up in a messy bun with spaghetti strands hanging down the sides of her cheeks.

"How could you leave us," she whispered, "when we needed you most?"

I couldn't speak. My lips moved, jaw flexed, but nothing came out. I tried. The muscles in my gut clenched and I exhaled, but was unable to explain why I left. Why I'd *had* to leave.

Jeanette stood, shifting again into someone more French, someone more male and bloodied and beaten, and slammed her fist down onto the table. "How could you leave us?" she screamed, knuckles crashing down until bits of bone and slivers of wood went flying. A pair of wire-thin glasses materialized over her eyes, one of which had begun to drift. "How could you leave us?" Her fist came down again on the heavy oak table, and now it shook the whole world around us, rattling plates and knocking glasses to the floor.

The banging continued, slicing through my subconscious, accompanied now with the sound of a buzzer. Someone calling my name. My full name, like my mother used to do when I did something stupid as a kid.

I sat up with a jerk, rubbing my eyes, looking around. Where the hell was I? It was night, a low light to my right swirling in the darkness. My computer's screen saver, multicolored strings twisting and mating on the LCD like a digital acid trip.

"Jarrod Nelson? Are you there? Open up, please."

I touched the mouse, the colors dissolved into the email I'd left open. My mother's message. The clock in the upper right hand corner read 20:42. Almost nine in the evening. I'd slept all day, even though the dream seemed to last only seconds.

"Coming," I said. The knocking continued, seeming to push through the door and into my chest. "Chill. I'm coming."

I flipped on the coffee maker as I shuffled to the door, and pulled on a pair of shorts. Through the peephole I saw a distorted image of a balding man in a spectacularly fine suit. Even this late at night, the suit pressed and boasting iron creases in all the right places.

This late at night, I thought.

"It's nine o'clock," I said. "What the hell do you want?"

"I would like to talk with you about Pierre Coudreau." Your voice silk, tempting. The devil's tone iced with a French accent.

"Hang on." I grabbed a shirt, this flimsy thing I had bought at a discount store in Pau that read *Freedom is a state of mine.* I'd thought it a clever saying, even though it had probably been the result of a poor translation or spelling error.

I saw the way you looked at it when I let you in. You squinted your eyes like it was a challenge, but I had simply grabbed whichever shirt was closest. You read too much into it.

"You must be Inspecteur Gerardy," I said.

"I must be," you said, half bowing and waving a hand before you. "And you are a difficult boy to make contact with."

I bristled at your use of the word *boy*. The French word—garçon—was considered an insult, unless you were speaking to a child. You don't even call your waiters garçon anymore.

You thought I didn't catch that?

"I'm terribly sorry if you were sleeping," you said. "May I come in?"

You were already moving before I stepped aside. Pulled up a seat, my only one, a cheap plastic picnic chair, and unbuttoned your jacket. Adjusted yourself for comfort. Looked like you planned on being here for a while.

I was still somewhere between asleep and awake, groggy and unsure if all this was actually happening or if I was in bed, dreaming you up.

"Is there something I can help you with, Inspecteur?"

You scanned my room before answering, taking particular notice of the map of Pau hanging on my wall, and pointing at it. "You have learned the town well?"

"Well enough to get to class and back."

"And the Boulevard des Pyrenees, I suspect." You said this with a grin and a nod, one finger against your nose, exposing that Palois belief that foreign students spent most of their free time—and even some of their class time—in the bars.

"I thought this was about Monsieur Coudreau," I said, acting brash, though I doubt you couldn't see through the mask. "My teacher."

You nodded again, straightening your smile, snuffing out the pretense. "It's just that I've spoken to everyone here already. Everyone except you."

"I was gone. Home in the United States."

"Oh?" Your face collapsed into wrinkles. "When did you return?"

"Day before yesterday."

"And when did you leave?"

"The day after—" I said on instinct, but caught the groove before derailing. "The day after exams." It won't hurt to tell you now that I'd almost admitted to leaving the day after Pierre died.

"Vacation?"

"My father had an accident."

You frowned, I remember it clearly, and said, "I'm sorry to hear that."

"About Pierre," I said, not wanting to talk about my father. A sort of melancholy lingered in my heart, exposed like a raw nerve when I thought too hard about the situation back home. "You were saying?"

You sighed. "Yes. About him. *C'est tragique.* But you must be used to such crime. You are from—?"

"Arizona."

"Yes, Arizona." You snapped your fingers. You knew this already but had misplaced the information. Or wanted me to believe you'd misplaced it. "Violence is common there, no?"

"No," I said, narrowing my gaze as if you were an encyclopedia salesman trying to sell me on the merits of being *smart* and *informed.*

"But you are close to Mexico, yes?"

"What does this have to do with Pierre?"

"Eh," you said, raising both hands in supplication. "*Calme toi.* I was only making conversation."

"Sorry. But it's late. I received bad news from home today. I don't have the time or patience for idle conversation."

"*Tu as raison,*" you said. "You're right." You stood, spitting on your knuckles and rubbing them against your chest. "I smell coffee."

I tasted my stomach. The implications of those three words—*I smell coffee.* They meant so much more than *Are you brewing coffee?* or *I* would *like some coffee, thanks.* They meant you weren't going anywhere anytime soon.

You flipped through some of my notebooks when I had my back turned. I'm sure of it. Might have even read my mother's email while I was pouring you a drink. What did you think you were going to find? A full confession with notes and timestamps?

"I am curious to know where you were on the evening of

Monsieur Coudreau's murder."

The pot slipped from my hand. Chipped the mouth of a cup. You had gone from casual to grave so quickly, it seemed the lights in my room had dimmed.

"I was with him," I said, without hesitation, sopping up the spill and beginning again.

You didn't blink. You thought you had me, didn't you?

"Go on," you said, lips curved downward like a loose rubber band.

"His sister and I were dating. Sort of."

"Sort of?"

"She had reservations."

"Her brother didn't like you?"

The lights muted a little more. You wore an expression that revealed nothing. It was not a blank, unknowing stare, but one that held secrets. You knew things, I was sure. You knew things you didn't want *me* to know.

"It wasn't that," I said.

"So what was it?"

"I was his student. Maybe he didn't want to breach that relationship. I don't know, really."

"And you met with him that night?"

"Caroline asked me to. She wanted me to make friends with him."

I served you coffee just the way you liked it, black with a pinch of sugar. You thanked me, even held the cup close and blew steam away from it, but you didn't take a drink. Not one.

"*Merci,*" you said, lifting the mug in salute.

You saw me flinch. You didn't know then why I did, but after reading about my confrontation in the shed with my father, you do now.

"So you were enemies?" you asked.

"I never said we were enemies."

"*Excuse-moi,* but if you are not friends, does that not make you enemies?" You shrugged, that impotent but all too

French gesture that could mean anything between *I don't get it* or *It's not my problem* or *I just don't care.* In this case, it meant you weren't playing games. I'll tell you now, and with no regret, your shrug just then—the mockery it withheld—made me want to scream.

"I was there to protect him," I said, sighing, at that point ready to tell you whatever necessary to get you out of my room.

"Protect him from what?"

From himself, I wanted to say, and though true, I realized how cliché it sounded. "He was studying gang mentality or something, got into some fights. So I had a drink with him at a bar downtown."

"So you were his . . . ah, what's the English word . . . his escort? Is that right?"

"I guess so."

"Did anything worth mentioning happen at this bar?"

I saw one of the secrets in your eye then, almost spelled out in capital letters. You already knew the answer, didn't you? You just wanted to see if I would lie.

"We . . ." I struggled to remember exactly how it had started. "We got into a fight."

"You and Pierre fought?"

"No," I said, too quickly adding, "I mean, not against each other. He was drunk, saying stupid things. Making people angry. So I paid for his drinks and got him out of there."

You saw me hesitate. "But?" you said.

"But one of them threw something or hit me. I . . . I can't really remember." It had only happened about a week ago. It bothered me that some of the details were already hard to place.

"And this is what happened to your head?"

I reached up without thinking, absently brushing the three-inch long scab, scratching the skin around it where the doctor had shaved my hair and sewed in the stitches.

"I took him home after that," I said.

"And then you left him?"

I remembered my dream, the vitriol in that same accusation coming from so many different mouths. I left. Yes, I left. Was I proud of it? Did it matter?

"Went straight home," I said.

"Home, here? Or home, United States?"

"Both." It was starting to feel good, this, telling you everything. It came out easier than I thought it would. "I was here at Theleme long enough to take a shower, then I left to catch a train for the airport."

You paused, stared at me long enough to make me self-conscious, almost to make me start talking again just to fill the space, then said, "These men at the bar. The ones you fought. Would you recognize any of them today, do you think?"

I tried to imagine them, but there were holes in the picture. Faces were unclear, wavy, like I was looking at them through water. "One of them was a skinhead." I thought hard enough to form a needle of pain behind my eyes, then shrugged.

"Do you recall the name of this place?"

"It didn't have a name, but . . ." I rifled through a jacket pocket and found the note Caroline had written down for me. "This is the address."

You looked at it, nodded, and handed it back. There it was, another secret. You already knew about the bar.

How the hell did you know about the bar?

"Monsieur Nelson," you said, rising, "I am happy for your cooperation so far, but I think there is . . ." You trailed off, circling your hands in search of just the right word. "More. Yes. I think there is something more. Something you are not saying."

"Whatever Roger told you is a lie. He's a scheming sack of shit."

I wished I hadn't said that.

You blinked. But it wasn't a blink of confusion, was it? It was one of triumph. "Roger?" you asked.

"Watford?"

"Oh. Yes. The Australian boy. Why would he lie? And what might he have to lie about?"

You were like a psychotherapist, questioning my conscience and trying to trick me into saying what you wanted to hear. Just so you know, I was onto you. Right then, I was onto you.

"Roger was jealous," I said. "He wanted to be with Caroline, but Caroline wanted to be with me. He probably told you I had something to do with it."

"He's said nothing of the sort. But it is interesting, no? That you believe he would say this?"

"Has he reported Caroline's disappearance?"

"Disappearance?"

I'll tell you now—because it's easier in print than in person—your habit of answering a question with a question made me want to punch myself. It was a different type of confrontation, less like you were questioning me, and more like you were forcing me to question myself.

"Caroline has gone missing," I said. "Roger—her flat mate, as you must know—told me she vanished after Pierre died. Didn't pack a bag. Took nothing."

You removed a moleskin from inside your jacket pocket, but your eyes remained locked on mine. "So Caroline . . . *disappeared* . . . approximately when you departed France. Is that correct?"

I started to feel sick again, the way you twisted the things I said to make them mean something else. To make them imply something sinister. "I guess it was around the same time."

As earlier, when your demeanor cold shifted from light-hearted to serious, you suddenly reversed again, smiling, rising and holding out your hand. "I thank you so much for your time, Monsieur Nelson. If you think of anything else, please call me. You still have my card. *Bonne nuit.*"

After you left, I dumped my cold stale coffee and poured a

fresh cup. And breathed. And saw the business card I had left on my desk. You must have been wondering why I didn't call you before you came knocking.

I had a funny feeling you and I weren't done with each other.

I sipped my coffee, thinking of Caroline and where she was at that moment. Was she alone? Was she sitting before a mirror, pulling her hair into a ponytail and scrubbing off makeup? Was she wondering whether she had done the right thing by going away? Was she wondering about me, and where I was at the moment? What I was doing?

"Don't be ridiculous," I said aloud. "Why would she spare a thought for you—or Roger, for that matter—right now?" She'd be thinking of her brother, trying to remember the last words she'd said to him, and regretting she hadn't said more.

SIXTEEN

I DIDN'T FALL IN love with Caroline that first night at Galway. Sparks didn't fly. She'd forced me to order several times, in French, and a different drink each time, but not even the alcohol we used as a study aid could temper my initial impression that she was selfish and thought quite a lot of herself. She had seemed distracted from the start, almost bored with my presence, rising at every opportunity to hug some friend of hers who happened to wander by the entrance.

The main interior of Galway was draped in shadows, perhaps to enhance the beer goggle effect, light coming from neon signs with red Carlsberg or brown Guinness or green Heineken logos. A long, sofa-like booth, covered in stretched and cracked vinyl, ran along the wall to the left. Drinkers leaned, elbows on the bar, or stood talking with their hands, since the stools had been moved to tables scattered throughout the main floor. We sat close to one of the windows so Caroline could occasionally primp herself in the reflection, and so I could see the entire layout of the place.

I couldn't stand to have anyone outside my line of sight, neither crowd nor single person. Call it lack of trust, call me over cautious. My father used to say, usually after a drink or six, to keep the door in sight and always sit where you could see the eyeballs of everyone in the room. That way, he said, no matter what happens, you'll never be caught dead under a table.

At one point, Caroline leaned over to a group nearby and introduced herself while I was practicing past-tense verb conjugations by running a list of everything I'd done the previous weekend.

"Aren't you here to help me study?" I asked, nudging her. "I know it's not the most stimulating conversation, but no one said a tutor's job was easy."

"Sorry," she said, not looking at me, but swiveling her head as if seeking someone more enthralling. "I thought I recognized that girl over there." She stuck a finger in her drink and swirled it around. "You were saying?"

"I was saying it seems kind of pointless if you're going to keep speaking to me in English."

She looked at me then, finely plucked eyebrows pinched together, and said something so quickly in French that I couldn't catch a word of it.

"Pretty sure that's not going to help either," I said.

I drained my glass, frustrated, ready to head back to my room, but something kept me in the chair, like there was an invisible wire between us—one end attached to her hip, the other to my fingertips. And Caroline, perhaps unintentionally but most likely not, reeled it in. Drawing me closer.

"Look," she said. "There's Roger."

Fucking Roger.

He used one hand to steady himself as he descended a staircase spiraling down from the restrooms. Caroline called to him over our little round table, scooting close to me to make space for him, and I felt the warmth of her thigh pressing against mine. Roger raised his pint in acknowledgement, and judging by the way he swayed, it wasn't the first. Probably not even the second or third.

They hugged. Kissed on the cheek, though it looked like he'd been aiming for her lips. Not for the first time—or the last—I wondered if they were an item. No, that's putting it too mildly. I wondered if they were fucking.

"This your first time here, mate?" he said, clasping my

hand in both of his. "Isn't it great?"

"It's a pub, alright," I said, pulling out of Roger's clammy grip.

"But don't you think it's funny? An Irish pub full of French people?"

"No funnier than one filled with Americans." He didn't hear. He was already talking over me.

"It's like some bad joke. A frog hops into an Irish—"

Caroline backhanded him in the chest. "You know how much I hate that term. *Frog*. What if I called you *kangaroo* or something?"

"If you eat frogs' legs," he said, "does that make you a cannibal?"

She hit him again, this time laughing, a sparkle brightening her dull green eyes. I was quickly becoming the odd man out.

"It seems our session is done today," I said. "I'm going to head home."

"No, man," Roger said, clutching my wrist and sliding his glass over. "Have a drink on me."

I looked into his pint, globs of foam and spittle floating around in there.

"No thanks," I said. "I don't know where your mouth has been."

Actually, I thought I *did* know where it had been.

He said something to Caroline in French, then hollered to the bartender.

Caroline leaned into my ear, said, "He won't let you leave until you have a shot with him."

Her lips brushed my ear as she spoke, tickling the tiny hairs there and tightening that invisible thread between us.

The bartender brought a tray with three more beers and a matching number of shot glasses overflowing with dark golden liquid. He struck a match, lit all three shots, then tossed his head back and made the universal *down the hatch* motion with finger and thumb.

"What is it?" I asked, gagging on the smell. Too many bad experiences with hard liquor in my past.

"Blow it out before you nail it," Roger said. "Unless you want to fry the fuzz off of your cheeks."

It was the first of many rounds that night. Precisely how many, who knew? But tray after tray of drinks appeared, and the edges gradually blurred around my vision. My lips seemed to swell, impairing my speech. My fascination with the perfect roundness of Caroline's cheekbones became preoccupation, then infatuation. I couldn't look away.

Snatches of time were sliced from memory like movie scenes left on the cutting room floor. In one scene, I'm pissing in the upstairs urinal at Galway.

Cut to black.

Fade in, I'm walking—arms extended out for balance—on the thin wall separating the boulevard and the sharp drop on the other side.

Cut to black.

Fade in, and I'm rounding a corner near L'Atomic Pizza. I see Roger and Caroline up against a wall, making out, his hand up her pink Miss Sixty blouse.

The churning in my stomach was part high grain alcohol, part jealousy. I left them there, slipping back toward the dorms without them knowing, my head spinning as I cut to black one final time.

I saw them again only the following evening, after the fog of my hangover had mostly moved on. With just coffee in my cabinets and sour smelling milk in my fridge, I stumbled outside to a rat hole of a pizza joint near my place.

Caroline and Roger were there, sharing a straw in the same glass of Coke. While I still moved slowly, trying not to reactivate the queasiness I'd felt only hours before, they were both cleansed and energetic, talking animatedly with chuckles and gregarious hand movements.

I had a vision of that kiss, of Roger copping a feel, and chased it into a closet in my mind. Had it even happened?

Had I imagined it? Had it been a drunken hallucination?

When I walked in, Caroline ran over and threw her arms around me.

"My God," she said, breathless. "You're okay."

She trembled, heart racing through her chest and into mine.

"Of course I'm okay." I reluctantly embraced her, enjoying the graze of her skin through a thin gray shirt, and relishing the sting of Roger's glare. "A bit rundown."

"We thought you were arrested," she said. "I've been knocking on your door all day."

"I was—" slightly ashamed that the drinks had hit *me* so much harder than *them*, so I said, "sleeping."

Roger stayed seated. Just stared, fingering a shaving of pepperoni into his mouth.

"Why would you think I was arrested?" I asked, not entirely sure I wanted to hear the answer.

"You don't remember?"

"Enlighten me. I certainly don't remember doing anything that would land me in jail. Did I piss in the street? Key someone's car?"

She glanced over at Roger. He said, "Go ahead, tell him," then turned away.

"You got into a fight," Caroline said.

"Busted the kid up pretty good," Roger added.

I shrugged out of Caroline's arms, headache returning, pins pushed into my temples as if someone somewhere was torturing a voodoo doll that looked like me.

"When?" I asked. "When did this happen?"

"We were all going home," Caroline said. "You disappeared and—"

She paused, glancing again at Roger, maybe considering which details to leave in and which to omit.

"—then we heard a commotion. Some guy was cursing at you, yelling, and someone else was shouting for him to stop."

"You had him on the ground when we got there," Roger said. "You saw us and ran."

"We tried to follow you," Caroline said, "but you were too fast. What happened, Jarrod?"

I shut my eyes and fought to open every closed door in my mind. There was nothing. That particular fragment of my life was gone, washed out by booze and anger and jealousy and a lack of self-control, probably forever.

SEVENTEEN

THE FOLLOWING MORNING, AFTER you and I met for the first time in my room, I saw Malcolm McCormack jogging across the lawn between the cafeteria and the faculté, smiling and waving at people he passed, and I thought he seemed well past stage four of grief.

It struck me as odd, this swift change from a couple of days ago, when he looked like someone had recently dug him up from his own grave. But death had never touched my life before. I'd never lost anyone. I guess anything more than a day or two of misery and sadness is just self-indulgent. Or it could be we're more resilient than we sometimes give ourselves credit for. We grieve, and then we move on. Because we have to.

I watched Malcolm pass through the faculté's filthy doors, the glass in them still scratched and gouged with protestations and the circle-A symbol for anarchy, residue from the latest greve against the system.

"If you think I look bad," I recalled him saying, "you should see her."

Audrey. Pierre's widow. The mother of his unborn child.

I tried to picture Audrey even though I had never seen her before, sobbing into her hands, head bobbing up and down as she gasped for breath, whispering to the bump in her stomach that everything was going to be okay, even though deep down she feared that nothing would be okay.

But instead of imagining Audrey doing those things,

saying those things, I saw Jeanette, with her coils of strawberry hair split and falling from a topknot, red icing smeared across the front of her baker's apron. I shook that vision away almost as soon as it manifested, afraid that it might've been truer than I was ready to accept.

If anyone would know where Caroline had gone, it would be Audrey. I still hoped that it was all a misunderstanding, that she'd simply needed to get away for a while. To escape this place that only brought memories of her brother. Nothing personal against me, nothing personal against Roger, even.

I understood the risk of returning to Pierre's apartment. I had seen the crime programs, the documentaries, heard the interviews with psychologists that spoke of how often a killer returned to the scene of the crime. They said it was because, as Pierre had suggested that night in the bar, we're not all sociopaths. Once regret and remorse slithered in, murderers often behaved—albeit unconsciously—as if they *wanted* to be caught.

So I knew what you would think if you saw me there. For Caroline, it was a risk worth taking. Especially if I was wrong. If something awful had happened to her, if she was hurt—or worse—I would never have been able to forgive myself.

As I approached the block of tenements where I'd left Pierre, something flapped in the wind, drawing my attention to the remnants of black and yellow police tape entwined in a fence nearby. Through a film of sweat dripping into my eyes, I saw two severed ends float up and slap together, the brief illusion of a person perched upon the fence, clapping. If I traced my steps back that way, back to where the crime had occurred, perhaps there would even be a chalk outline—or had that become so antiquated that it was only ever seen in movies?

I palmed the sweat away. Daylight seemed to draw thin and transparent, almost painful, the closer I came to the building. I was reminded of those old block factories I used to see in Phoenix, back before the economy turned into an atrophied muscle. Three-stories high, windows stacked on windows beside more windows, most of them covered with shades that looked more like carpets than curtains. Brick walls so weathered by rain as to be almost black with mildew and mold.

To think Audrey would have to raise her child, alone, in such a place. The first—and the last—time I'd been there, the night had covered up the cracks in the paint, the blemishes on the skin. This area was much more depressing in daylight.

A man dressed smartly in slacks and professor's coat, black fedora like a dirty halo atop his head, appeared from an alley between two of the blocks and walked quickly toward the door to Pierre's building. I shielded my eyes from sunlight refracting off of all those glassy eyes, thinking the guy looked familiar. No, he didn't *look* familiar, but he did move familiarly. He seemed slow on one side, dragging a leg or limping a little. Had I caught a glimpse of him that night, nothing more than a flash as Pierre and I fled occupied with more pressing concerns, but seeing the man just long enough for him to be burned into my subconscious?

He slipped a key into the front door lock and grasped the doorknob. His hand turned, but the doorknob didn't. He stepped forward as if the door had opened, but it hadn't, and then he moved right through it. A few seconds later, the door swung open from the inside.

A prickly sensation walked up my back, an invisible tattoo artist working on my spine.

My vision swam again, sunlight washed away behind clouds, the bright watercolor of golds and reds and greens muted back into reality.

The door was already open, you fool. You're not seeing ghosts. You're not . . .

"Seeing ghosts," I said. I repeated the mantra, pressing the door the rest of the way open, noticing the jamb was split as if someone had pried it open with a crowbar. I held my breath, stepped inside.

The man had crested a staircase just off to the left of the main hallway. He appeared solid and full of life, though most likely deaf or hard of hearing. I called up to him again, a little louder this time.

"*Excuse-moi, monsieur. Vous connaissez Madame Coudreau?*"

He paused and shuffled to the right—which was strange since the staircase cut a sharp angle to the left—faced the wall and then continued around as if the movement caused pain in the left side of his body. And when he leveled his gaze at me, I fell back against the door in shock because one eye fell upon me and the other drifted off on its own accord.

I sucked air through my teeth and held it there. The man at the top of the stairs was my father. In that brief moment of lucidity, I would have sworn on it.

But the moment passed. I exhaled, blinked. Of course it wasn't him. This man's bad eye was rheumy, diseased, his face weathered and stretched across his skull like dried leather. He pointed at his ear, shrugged, then disappeared up the stairs.

I didn't get it then, but I see it now after all that has happened. It was a sign, right? I shouldn't have been there. But I followed that old guy up the stairs, cringing at every creak and groan of settling wood, maybe even distantly telling myself—screaming at myself—that something wasn't right.

The staircase curved farther up to a linoleum hallway that stretched off to the left. The angles where the floor met the wall were all wrong, mismatched, the baseboards warped and in places showing several layers of old paint. At the far end, shrouded in a hazy, ghost-like light, the man's apartment door swung shut. To the right, a window overlooking a small, green courtyard behind the building.

The glass foggy, spotted with grime. A car, dark chocolaty brown in color, idled outside.

From somewhere down the hallway—not the old guy's apartment, I was certain, but closer—more noises. Something like a hand rustling through a silverware drawer. The clatter of cabinets opened and slammed shut. Mattresses pulled up and dropped heavily on the frame. Hangers rattling around in closets.

From my subconscious, more warnings.

The car outside blew its horn, a sharp blat that made me jump and turn back to the window.

The apartment door nearest me slammed open a fraction of a second before a reflection flashed across the window. I turned halfway—no time to think, no time to speak—before feeling the ballpoint of a shoulder smashing me against the wall, breath shot from my lungs like a deflating tire. The wound on the back of my head reignited and I fell to my knees, struggling to see through stars. He took the stairs down two at a time, then rounded the ground floor hallway at a sprint, almost falling, in the opposite direction from which I had entered.

I pulled myself up, struggling to breathe, and leaned on the windowsill. The guy shot out of a back door. Within moments he was in the car, and they were gone.

I should have left, but curiosity drew me toward the door he'd burst through, the door creeping back to closed after its impact against the wall. A worm of dread burrowing in my gut, I saw the name inscribed above the doorbell.

Coudreau.

EIGHTEEN

THE GIRL FROM DOWN the hall, the one who wore the same purple and red striped stockings every day, said someone had been at my door again while I was away, knocking and ringing the bell for several minutes. Wasn't a cop, she'd said, though he sure was dressed like he had somewhere important to go.

Was that you, I wonder?

I switched off the bedside lamp and sat at my window, shock and physical pain finally wearing off. It had begun to rain just after I came inside, wind crashing violently against the shutters like marching band drums. From there, up on the fourth floor, I saw wrist-thick branches ripped from trees and thrown into parked cars along the street. A garbage can skipped along the sidewalk, its repetitive clang of metal on concrete barely audible over the sudden storm. As the clouds swept in and darkened the world, a mangy dog cowered and shivered under the front steps of a bakery across the road.

I tried to shut it all out. Made my mind a chalkboard, wiped it clean of all distraction. Sank into that place of Zen, a rational and focused and objective state of being to which I gave a voice and a name: Izzy. My Inner Zen Therapist.

You think I don't know how crazy that sounds?

Izzy flipped on a projector that beamed a cone of light at the chalkboard, and replayed the stairway scene.

The image paused in mid-jump, a second or two after I'd been shouldered into the wall, just as the man was fleeing down the stairs. I gauged his height and weight—five-elevenish, a buck-seventy—right around Roger's. And the smell, that of someone who'd been drinking for days, that stink of booze squeezing from his pores like sweat. Too familiar to be coincidence.

But what was he doing at Audrey's apartment?

"He was planting evidence, just like he planted Pierre's wallet and glasses."

I broke out of my meditation and searched my pockets. Nothing was missing. ID card was there, what little money I had was there. But that meant nothing. All he needed was something with my name on it, something that could be traced back to me.

What if he snatched my receipt from the Italian restaurant that night? The last time I saw Caroline. He's jealous of me. He's been planning this for a while.

That was an ironic bit of turnabout. Roger jealous of me.

I switched on my laptop and directed the web browser first to the BBC site with localized French content. On the main page—*University Professor Murdered.* The report was only a day old, and mentioned nothing about Pierre's missing sister.

I navigated to a different site, Pau's online newspaper, with more recent revelations. Breaking news about the wallet and the glasses. I had to run the text through a translator to get all the details, but again, no mention of Caroline, other than a footnote: *Immediate family could not be reached for comment.*

Wouldn't that make news? Wouldn't some excitable reporter be keen to link Caroline's disappearance with her brother's murder?

Of course they would. Which meant only one thing.

"Roger's lying," I said. "He knows where she is."

He wasn't clever enough to have planned all this out. He was an opportunist. He had inside information from Caroline —that I was with Pierre that night, that I'd left the next day

—and he saw an opening, a tiny fracture he could wedge his fingers into and pry wide. Pierre, notoriously resistant to his little sister dating foreigners, was already out of the way. Now, with a little manipulation, a little groundwork, he had set to work on me.

Love does crazy things to people. *Love,* my father used to say, *is what makes me hit you, boy.*

What had love done to Roger?

NINETEEN

THE STORM HAD MOVED on, gray skies splitting open for a hot summer sun that dried muddy soil and soggy leaves within an hour or two. I crossed a parking lot behind the Champion supermarket, gaggles of children already skipping back outside to kick a ball around in the field next door. A few boys stomped across the grass, one of them chipping a soccer ball to my feet. I laid into it, arcing the ball well above and beyond them and they cheered, chasing after.

But a few of them, I noticed, simply stood and stared as I passed the field and the synagogue nearby, out to the street that led into town.

On the main road, a car heading south—the same as me—toward the mountains, pulled over. The passenger's side window slid down and the driver leaned over, asking me for directions. His wife averted her eyes and punched his leg. He responded sharply to her, then drove off without another word.

I stopped, looking myself over. Was there something wrong with me? Something that caught those kids' attention? Something that caused the woman just now to look away from me with apprehension, and then insist her husband drive on?

The closer I came to Roger's and Caroline's apartment, the more I noticed people slowing as I passed by them. Cars veering slightly away from the sidewalk I traveled on. Fenced in dogs barking as I crossed in front of their yards.

When I was younger, before reality television moved from pop culture phenomenon into a psychological study of human behavior, I used to pretend that the whole world was watching me. I adjusted my posture, the way I moved, the way I spoke, all in an effort to project a certain impression upon people. I wanted them to think I was infallible, strong and confident, aware of—but not overly concerned with—my appearance, when in truth, my whole identity was fake.

Now, I had that same impression, that everyone was watching, only more intensely. As a kid, as much as I wanted to be the center of attention, I always knew I wasn't. People were too concerned with their own preoccupations, their own responsibilities. Maybe they even thought the whole world was watching *them*.

It's just an impression, I told myself now. *An old habit.*

When I finally reached Caroline's flat, not in fear of meeting Roger there now but in hopes of finding him, I caught a blur of activity, a face vanishing from around the corner as I reached out to buzz the doorbell, like someone had been waiting to see if I would return.

Roger, I thought.

I wrestled down the urge to shout after him.

From that direction, juvenile laughter, adults singing *Allez les Bleus,* stray dogs barking and clacking their nails against cobblestone streets.

Only early in the afternoon, with hours yet until the game, there were more people gathered in Place Clemenceau than I'd expected. Three theater-sized projection screens had been mounted on the far side of the square, draped over by heavy blue tarps in case the rain rolled back in. Along the edges of the common, beverage carts were manned by pretty young girls, their high cheekbones painted red, white, and blue, wearing sultry smiles and looking ready to trade phone numbers for drinks.

Everywhere I looked, flesh. No familiar faces. No one paid any particular attention to me here, but standing at the mouth of this crowd, with police officers posted in obvious locations and certainly a few more hidden, I suddenly felt an oppressive sense of exposure, like those dreams where you arrive at school to the laughter of your classmates, only to look down and realize you're stark ass naked.

Do you have those dreams too? Or are they cultural, would you say? I believe we build these images of ourselves, like I did as a kid, presenting ourselves in a certain way, the way we may not necessarily be but the way we *want* to be, and those dreams represent a deeply rooted fear that people will see through our masks to who we really are.

Rather than run away and draw further attention to myself, I put on that disguise and strode into the crowd as if I belonged there. I shoved my hands in my pockets to appear casual and relaxed, even though I was actually hiding the nervous twitch in my fingers. No sudden movements. Level gaze. But aware and on the lookout for Roger, or anyone who seemed to be on the lookout for me.

On the far side of Place Clemenceau, just before I passed under the three giant screens, someone switched on the projectors to test the signal. For a few seconds, through black and white snow and the rapid-fire blare of buzz and feedback over the loudspeakers, I thought I heard a voice buried in there somewhere, struggling to be heard over the noise. The center screen went clear, the left, then the right, and I glanced quickly away, nauseated.

A low cheer erupted as the images presumably showed highlights from the previous rugby World Cup matches. France had done surprisingly well so far, easily plowing through the elimination rounds. A win against the legendary All Blacks would knock New Zealand—heavy favorites— from the competition, and would give the nation an excuse to celebrate and drink and cause a sort of subdued mayhem. But with one bad play, with one lost ball, the fever could easily become fury.

But I still couldn't look at the screens.

I continued through the crowd, in the direction of the train station and the Boulevard des Pyrenees, anxiety rising with the pulse of the masses. They seemed to have all melted together into one giant sinister creature, multi-headed, limbs stretched out like threads in a dream catcher, hands slipping in and out of unsuspecting pockets. The air tasted heavy, like sulfur. People were blowing off fireworks. I couldn't breathe.

The boulevard opened up and hordes of people were already excitedly jumping on moving vehicles as they inched down the street. I swallowed lungfuls of oxygen, dizzy now, desperately searching for a gap, a hole out of this creature's stomach. There were hundreds of them, so close and packed together that I couldn't tell which heads belonged to which bodies. I elbowed, I shouldered. Soon enough I began swinging, yelling, feeling a hundred hands and hips and asses crushing against me, and I struggled through, aiming for a waist-high wall that ran along the edge of the boulevard. Beyond it, space, as the land dropped away at a sharp incline leading toward the train station below.

I found a place at the wall and created a bubble—no skin within arm's reach of me. Leaning forward, chest burning, not thinking straight. Feeling like diving over the wall and tumbling down the hill and just collapsing wherever I landed.

"Hey, my man," someone said behind me. "You alright?" The guy looked familiar, thick dreadlocks shooting out from underneath a colorful Rastafarian knit cap, but I couldn't place him at first.

"I don't like crowds."

"Guess this isn't the best place for you, then."

"Do I know you?"

"Wanna get high?"

It clicked. Another American student. He'd come down on the bus with us from Paris. A first name that sounded more like a last. Francis or Fernandez or Francisco, maybe.

"A bunch of us went to Morocco last weekend, man. Got

fucked up." He gave the word *fucked* a few extra syllables for emphasis. "Came back with some good shit, too."

Somewhere in the blurry recesses of memory, a door opened and I caught a glimpse of Roger and this guy sharing a table and a beer at Café Russe, the Russian bar right on the other side of the boulevard.

"You seen Roger around?" I asked.

"Watford? Aussie kid? Yeah, he was at the Galway, like, five minutes ago. With Fanny. You know Fanny? Hot. Great ass. Perfect name."

I looked over Francis's or Fernandez's or Francisco's shoulder to the strip of pubs behind him. Shining like a beacon, a Galway sign in the neon green of a radioactive four-leaf clover.

"So, man," he said as I pushed past him. "Wanna get high?"

TWENTY

I KNEW FANNY. I'D known her since my first day in Pau. I knew the slink in her walk, how the heat from her body made it feel like you were standing next to a fireplace, and how her practiced focus on a person's lips could make them reveal secrets.

Fanny never hid her obsession with foreigners. She'd tagged along with our group during our initial campus tour, skipping from guy to guy, linking arms and telling all who would listen that her name was also her favorite body part. One of the more local study abroad students—a vulgar English hooligan with perfectly feathered blond hair and a fixation on barely legal actresses, a guy who'd repeatedly failed his classes, but only barely, and on purpose, so he could stay in the country longer—had warned me about Fanny. He'd told me to watch my head. Called her a "modern day Marie Antoinette," whatever that was supposed to mean.

The first time I'd seen her she was sitting on the curb, bruised knees almost up to her ears, when our bus pulled up outside the dorms. Our first evening in Pau, actually, since we had rolled in sometime near midnight. And already she was there.

A black-haired girl with bright red lipstick and eyes as cold and as deep as a pair of graves.

She weaseled her way into every party or gathering in the dorms, showing up even if no one knew who she was, flirting and friendly with everyone under the pretense of teaching how to get along in her country without looking like an outsider. Making friends with everyone but me, that was, since I was fresh from Arizona and already aching, having just left Jeanette, having thrust myself into this strange place where everything seemed the same but nothing really was.

But she caught me, in less than a week, shadowing while I walked from Theleme to a restaurant I'd soon dub The Best Worst Pizza In Europe. I kept my eyes low, counting the cracks in the sidewalk, trying not to make myself obvious, trying not to let her know how my blood stirred when I saw her hips swaying. She'd worn black tights and white tennis shoes. A low-cut t-shirt that read I AM NOT YOUR SLAVE.

None of the employees at the restaurant spoke English. I ordered a bottle of wine—that much I knew how to ask for—and the girl behind the counter giggled, mocking my pronunciation.

"*Oon bouteyaoo doo vaahn,*" she'd said, calling to the guys ladling sauce and rolling dough behind her. "*Autre chose?*"

I pointed to the menu above her head. Tried to sound out the name of the pizza I wanted.

"*Pardon?*" she said, not getting it, but still laughing.

"Never mind." My face burned with embarrassment. "Fuck you and your pizza," I said, knowing they wouldn't understand.

That dark haired specter stood behind me, blocking my retreat.

"What do you want?" she asked. "I'll order for you." Her accent was of that sultry, silky variety heard in old movies on the International Film Network.

I shared my dinner and wine with her. Felt obliged to. She told me her name was Fanny.

"You know," she said, grinning. "Like *ass.*"

* * *

I wasn't particularly surprised to hear about Fanny spending time with Roger, who I'd once overheard introduce himself as "hard drinking, hard headed, and hard fucking." I spotted them right away, at a table al fresco and alone, smiles lubricated and pint glasses lined up. The sound of their voices an incomprehensible thread in the general din. Roger made hand motions and pursed his lips as if whistling. Fanny pushed him and laughed. When she reached out, her hand lingered briefly on his chest before pulling away.

I doubted they were commiserating over Roger's missing roommate. Or Caroline's dead brother.

The sidewalk on that edge of the boulevard cut right through the cluster of tables outside the bars. I circled around in the direction of Place Clemenceau, from where I'd come, then doubled back along the sidewalk.

A scuffed and muddied soccer ball rolled toward me, weaving between legs and stopping at my feet. The people around me seemed to slow, their conversations dragging as if this were a movie and someone was pressing a thumb down on the film as it ran. I blinked hard, that same sense of breathless vertigo I sometimes got after a workout when my blood sugar was low. I bent down to pick up the ball. Someone stepped forward and snatched it out of my hands.

"This baby's mine now," the person said in passing, tongue flicking out hungrily, his words hot and minty in my ear.

I knew that voice. I looked up just in time to see his teeth ground together, dark yellow stains at the roots. He was there, in my face, and then he was gone just as quickly, a snapshot amongst this slow moving crowd.

I stumbled, horrified, knowing Mario was in Arizona, probably with Jeanette, but as certain as death that he'd been right in front of me right then. There was even a faint scent of coconut shampoo in the air, the same shampoo he'd used every day since I had known him. It had become his signature smell.

Time crept back up to normal speed. I looked for Mario but he had gone, melted back into the crowd.

"No," I said. "He wasn't there."

But he *could've* been there. I mean, it wasn't entirely impossible. And if he *was* here in France, was Jeanette here too? Wouldn't that be funny if, as was Jeanette's dream, they had come to get married?

It wouldn't be funny at all.

A woman in red heels and matching miniskirt heard me talking to myself and laughed.

I needed to sit. I needed food and rest and I needed to think. But thinking hurt. The gash in the back of my head started to throb, to itch, and I wondered if it had opened up. This wasn't right. *I* wasn't right. I felt like a doll, sewn up from crotch to throat, Arizona pulling at one half and France pulling at the other and me somewhere in between, the seams slowly ripping apart.

I leaned up against a barricade, closed my eyes until the sky stopped tumbling, until I felt I could open them again without passing out. Someone at a nearby table leaned over and asked if I was okay, handing me a plastic cup of water. I thanked him, handed the cup back, and saw Roger a few tables away, watching me.

The smile on his face faltered as he scooted his chair back, said something hastily to Fanny, and fled into the crowd.

I couldn't run, but climbed over the barrier separating sidewalk and curb, right into the street where traffic was at a near standstill. Rowdy rugby fans continued to harass cars as they idled by, but there was slightly more room on the bicycle path. Roger had taken off in the direction of Henri the Fourth's chateau, and though I'd already lost sight of him, I followed the commotion left in his wake. Curses. Spilled beers. Sudden shouts of surprise or anger.

He was running, so I chased him.

The crowd thinned as we escaped the bar strip. Roger had about fifty yards on me when he cut a right down Place

Royale, and if he made it further into town it would be too easy to lose him among the web of interconnecting roads and sidewalks. I came to the corner, slowly regaining my composure, hearing those words *This baby's mine now* again in my head, and I couldn't tell if the voice was Mario's or Roger's.

The park was a stark contrast to the busy street we'd left behind. Relatively quiet, almost completely void of people. A young couple quietly kissed up against a tree, oblivious to everything but the pounding of their hearts and the wetness of their tongues. An older man strolled with hands clasped behind his back, a leash wrapped around one wrist and a sparkling white Pomeranian ahead of him sniffing along the curb.

I stole into the park, sunlight fading behind gray cloud cover, a pinprick rain beginning to fall. Black silhouettes pasted like cutouts against the dark blue background of nightfall.

There were rows of trees, limbs twisted and awkward but all forming the same shapes, with wires discreetly attached to redirect the growth patterns. They framed a manmade pond and a statue of Henri at one end, the spotlighted façade of the mayor's office on the other. I moved from shadow to shadow.

"I know you're here somewhere," I said, evenly, restraining the temptation to yell. "Just come out, yeah? Let's talk."

I held my breath, heard the crack of a twig, and the muffled exhalation of a hunted animal. A footstep. I crouched low, sliding across the shoulder width road, moving behind a line of parked cars, dropping into the gaps between tiny European vehicles and hulking, imported SUVs. The acrid stink of petrol and worn rubber in my nose. The bumper of a black Audi was still warm.

"Where's Caroline, Roger?"

No reply, but for the wind singing with a shriek.

"She didn't send the text, did she? *Don't come back to France?* That was *you*, wasn't it?"

Nothing.

"What were you doing at Audrey's?" I asked.

A small gang of hipsters, drunk and slurring and playing French hip-hop through the tinny speaker of a cell phone, answered my question with a string of harsh phrases my language teacher had warned us to never use in public. After they danced their way to the boulevard and around the corner, I stood and called Roger's name.

But he was gone.

France won the match that night, as I'm sure you remember, infecting the masses with a national pride ferocious enough to incite rampant vandalism. Whether or not they would go on to win the whole thing didn't matter at that point. They'd beaten the best the world had to offer, which, for many of the fans, provided a fantastic excuse to get wasted and destroy things.

It also meant you were too busy dealing with them to bother with me.

So instead of heading home or sticking around Place Clemenceau to watch the chaos unfold, I went straight back to Caroline's apartment, made myself comfortable on a mound of grass across the way, and waited.

The entire country suffered a hangover in the morning, the stench of vomit and regrettable sexual liaisons in the air. Streets were littered with car antennas and crushed beer cans and shards of glass. Boulangeries opened late, their owners muttering, making deals with God, promising to never touch a bottle of wine again as long as they lived.

Roger hadn't come home, and I'd seen no lights or shadowy figures moving behind the windows. He'd probably spent the night with Fanny, if not with Caroline, wherever she was.

I jogged the mile or so back to the dorms, forcing myself into activity, slowing to a walk when passing any vehicle that looked like it might be one of yours. But instead of going home, I cut a right toward the campus, relishing the warm blood flooding my veins.

Grasses were neon, the sky was so blue I had to squint. I felt like I'd spent the last week walking through a fog, and now the sunlight was finally burning it off. But it was only extreme exhaustion, when the body and mind are so close to shutting down that everything appears vivid and surreal, bright and colorful. I was no closer to finding Caroline, no closer to answers of any kind. The entire night had unfolded in such an absurd, almost hallucinogenic fashion, I wondered if there wasn't something seriously wrong with my head. Mario in France, and Jeanette with him? To get married? Why would they do that? Out of spite? To fuck with me even more? Were they conspiring against me because I left Jeanette while she was pregnant, and didn't even bother to ask her whose kid it was?

Were they *all* conspiring against me, Roger and Caroline too because I let Pierre die? And you, goddammit, letting this play out . . . for what? For your own pleasure? Because you had nothing else to go on? When would it end? When you found Pierre's killer? Even then, would it end? Would I still be haunted by the idea that I had somehow caused it? That it was my fault for fighting in the bar? That it was my fault for going there in the first place? That it was my fault for wanting to prove to Caroline I could take care of her? That it was my fault for needing to play the hero?

Very simply, that it was my fault?

TWENTY-ONE

DO YOU REALLY LOVE her? Caroline, I mean.
"Yes."
You don't sound so sure.
"YES, I FUCKING LOVE HER."
No need to be crass.
"Sorry."
Can you imagine life without her?
"I suppose so."
Then she's Roger's baby now. What about Jeanette?
"What about Jeanette?"
How do you feel about her being pregnant?
"Afraid."
Fear is a generic emotion. HOW DO YOU FEEL?
"I feel sick."
Because the child might be yours?
"I don't love her. It wouldn't be fair."
It wouldn't be fair to Jeanette? Or the child? Or you?
"All three."
Don't bullshit yourself.
"Okay. So I don't want a kid. Is that so selfish?"
Then she's Mario's baby now. What about Pierre?
"What about Pierre's baby?"
What about Pierre?
"What about Pierre?"
Why did you do it?
"Why did I leave him?"

If that's what you prefer to call it.
"That's what it was."
That's not all it was.
"He was stubborn. Drunk."
You can't lie to yourself forever.
"What do you want me to say?"
Say what's in your heart.

TWENTY-TWO

MY EMAIL PINGED AND I sat up, the words "Say what's in your heart" on my lips, everything before that receding, fading away like pictures drawn in condensation. My first foggy thought was that the last couple of days hadn't happened, and I was living again—for the first time—the night you stopped by, interrupting my sleep with your questions, your thinly veiled accusations. I half-expected you to knock on my door just then. In fact, I got up and double-checked the lock, *certain* you were there.

My clock even read the same time as before. 20:42.

I waited for you, waited until 21:15, and then realized I was being foolish. So I checked my email, hoping it wasn't more bad news from my mother. Hoping it was from Caroline.

The address line read Pierre@Coudreau.net, with a blank space where the subject should have been. The message itself was only one sentence long, and unsigned.

Thought you'd get away with it, didn't you?

I tapped out and sent a response, the first words that came to mind, without considering whether or not it was a good idea to engage in this game.

What did I get away with?

The message had to have come from Roger, using a bogus domain name. He was trying to scare me. Did he think I'd be so stupid to condemn myself in messages he could print out and give to you?

"This isn't going to end," I said aloud. "He's going to keep on me and on me until I stop him or until I go insane."

I switched on the coffee maker, realizing I had been practically injecting this stuff lately, staying awake through the night and sleeping all day, turning my life inside out and my reality into something tenuous. It was going to be hell when classes started up again.

How could I even think of going to class, or assuming any kind of normal routine, amidst all this?

The email client pinged again, but it wasn't a reply from Roger. My message had bounced back from the *mailer-daemon* with an explanation for why the delivery had failed.

The address Pierre@Coudreau.net does not exist.

"Not possible," I said, checking the first message again, that sense of unreality becoming more unbearable, like the floor might next fall out from beneath my feet.

Could Roger have disabled the account already? Could he have blocked any incoming emails from my address? Neither scenario seemed likely. What would've been the point? Did he really expect me to believe Pierre Coudreau was contacting me from the grave, and via the Internet, no less?

AOL, I thought, laughing. *Apparitions On Line.*

But then another email came through from the same name.

Liar, it read. *You're a goddamned liar.*

I tried to reply again, stabbing harder at the keys this time like you do when you *really fucking mean it*, but then another message pinged, then another, and more, popping into the queue every second and filling up the screen, scrolling it downward until that dead address was all I could see. The cache of unread emails kept growing and growing, so fast that the upward ticking number of new messages began to blur.

I slammed the lid of my computer shut so hard I heard something crack inside.

TWENTY-THREE

I LEFT MY ROOM—without opening my laptop before—disgusted that I'd let Roger push my buttons, that I'd let myself lose such control. I had seen him in the university computer lab, both before and after classes some days, typing away in what looked like code. And just now, he'd probably been hiding out somewhere, hacking into my computer, running it remotely. I ran a mental checklist of all the emails I'd sent, all the Internet searches I'd done since learning of Pierre's death, trying to remember if there was anything incriminating in there. Anything he could use against me.

And he *should* be hiding out after last night. If he had any sense at all, he'd disappear for a while.

So Fanny was my last resort. At some point, Pierre would have come up in their conversation. This otherwise boring town had been injected with a dose of drama, and everyone was talking about it. If Roger had even suggested that there were rumors or gossip of my involvement, Fanny would have teased every last detail out of him.

She has a way with boys, I may have mentioned that.

After the previous night's festivities, I suspected the bars would be mostly empty. Pau had a population somewhere in the hundred thousand range, so the chances of randomly crossing Fanny's path were slim. And Fanny seemed to appear and disappear at will anyway, another ghost, lured by the scent of foreign testosterone. Still, I'd have a better chance of finding her than finding Roger.

I started at the only other place I knew foreign students hung out; a small theater that showed international films in their native languages. This place was tucked well away, practically in the suburbs. Like the nameless bar where Pierre and I had shared our first and last drinks, the theater was easily missed if you didn't know what you were looking for. It was a converted house, practically a shack, crab grass growing around the base, run by a couple of aficionados who had gone to film school. Purists. Anarchists. Highly anti-capitalist. They didn't believe in advertising, only word of mouth. If you were curious enough to duck your head inside a cramped alcove in that doorway you would see a tattered sheet of paper with the week's show times.

I checked my watch, ran a finger down the list. The last film of the evening was just about to let out.

At the sound of voices and commotion inside, I hid behind a telephone booth across the street. A truck with its headlights on low rolled by. Laughter rose from inside the theater foyer, followed by a contagious racking of coughs that jumped from person to person.

The doors opened and a small group trickled out, waving through a fog of smoke that poured out with them. I recognized no one until the Rasta kid I had seen the day before, smoke coiled around him like a burned out aura. He flicked a renegade dreadlock over his shoulder, turned and bent away from a streetlight, and lit up a cigarette. He caught the door, pulled it open. Passed the cigarette to the next person who came out.

Fanny.

I waited, watching the light swirl through smoke like a dream, acutely aware that people, these days, walked into my life—for better or worse—right when I needed them to.

But what shook me was the woman behind Fanny, eyes shifting from left to right, wearing Adidas trainers and a formless black top. She had those high cheekbones and a glint in her eye that reminded me of Caroline, but this woman's hair was much longer, curled, and strawberry red. No makeup covering the freckles on her nose. It was like someone had taken a photograph of Jeanette and superimposed it over Caroline's face, melding their best features to create a vision so striking I lost the strength in my knees.

I reached out, planted a palm on the phone booth to hold myself up, when I saw Roger coming out of the theater. Smoke still seemed to flow out through the doors behind them, and the whole scene was so implausible—all of them together, right there and right then—that I hadn't noticed Francis or Fernandez or Francisco pulling up in a rusted Ford hatchback that had been parked down the street.

I moved out of the darkness.

"Caroline," I said. It wasn't much more than a whisper.

The woman didn't respond or even acknowledge my presence, but Roger saw me, pushed her into the backseat and climbed in after her, shouting, "*Allez, Fabian. Maintenant!*"

The car sped off before I could even think of chasing, leaving Fanny and I there, staring at each other awkwardly, in the middle of the street.

TWENTY-FOUR

"WANT SOME?" SHE ASKED, blowing translucent rings from her pursed lips and holding the cigarette out.

"I don't smoke."

The Ford hatchback had taken a sharp left, screeching its tires, heading toward the main avenue. I tried to match Fabian's car to the vehicle that had fled from Pierre's apartment, but there were too many small cars in this small country, and they all looked alike. But I was certain of one thing.

They both had the same dark chocolaty paint job, which was close enough for me.

"I should have brought a jacket," Fanny said, sidling closer. Shivering. Glancing down the road where Fabian had screamed off. "What was that all about?"

"Why don't you tell me?"

"How should I know?" She lowered her eyelashes, tried to slide a hand around my waist. I batted it away. Fanny pouted.

"I didn't know you were friends with Caroline."

"Caroline?"

"Pierre's sister," I said. "Roger's roommate. You know goddamned well who."

She inhaled deeply on the cigarette, a red-hot cherry of ash lighting her cheeks orange. She puckered. Breathed smoke into my face. "Her?" she said. "Her name is Vanessa."

I stepped back, onto the sidewalk, retreating from her

toxic cloud. "You think I'm stupid."

"I think you're sexy. You work out."

"Don't fuck with me."

"If you fuck with me, maybe I'll tell you something."

Cool wind came rushing through the intersection, vacuuming between rows of houses, rattling street signs, cutting through the white cloud that still seemed to be hovering around the theater, and making Fanny shiver again and dare to come closer. She curved an arm around me and I let her this time.

I thought about Caroline, so quick to run away after I'd visited my father in Arizona, like she'd just been waiting for a reason. How she'd ignored me—yes, *ignored,* that was the right word—just now. How she'd apparently sought her comfort and solace in Roger's arms as soon as the opportunity presented itself. As soon as I let her down. As soon as I let her brother die.

The gentle brush of Fanny's fingertips tickled up and down the small of my back. I almost wanted to fuck her out of spite.

So I kissed her, slightly revolted at the taste of tar and nicotine on her tongue, but turned on because I knew it was wrong. She was short. I grabbed a fistful of hair and tugged her head back. She moaned into my mouth, standing on her toes as she angled her face up to mine.

"What did he tell you?" I said, as Fanny sunk her teeth lightly into my neck. "That I had something to do with it?"

"To do with what?" she said, the warmth from her breath sparking across my flesh like electricity.

"Pierre. Did he tell you I did it?"

"I don't know what you're talking about."

"Who's Vanessa?"

"Just some girl."

I pulled Fanny beneath an overhang, into the shadows, exploring every bit of her exposed flesh. I couldn't think straight, couldn't tell if she was lying. We folded deeper into the darkness as a man walked by, huddled in his pea coat to combat the rising wind.

"*Oh la la*," he said, spotting us. "*Viva l'amour.*"

We must have pawed each other for five or ten seconds more, completely mindless and awash in hormones, lost in the divine rush of The First Kiss. It's a drug. A special sort of high people destroy their marriages, their families, sometimes their lives, in pursuit of.

I opened my eyes and the man was still there, just a few feet away. Watching with hands shoved deep in his pockets, one of them moving obscenely up and down.

"Don't stop on my account," he said, the other hand drunkenly rising to push a pair of wire-rimmed glasses up the bridge of his nose. "Please."

"Jesus Christ," I said, pushing Fanny off of me.

"Hey," she said, covering her mouth. Her palm came away with blood. "I think you bit me."

"What the hell is wrong with you, man?"

"He's just some homeless guy," Fanny said, narrowing her eyes at me. "What is wrong with *you?*"

"*Pardon*," he said, pulling both hands from his pockets and holding them in the air, like a criminal suspect pleading ignorance, bushy eyebrows spiked with concern and maybe a little fear. "*S'il vous plait, pardon.*"

He shuffled off, and the brief, uncontrollable urge that had connected Fanny and I for a moment was gone. I watched the man grow smaller in the distance, seeming to wink in and out of existence as he moved from streetlamp to streetlamp. Fanny lingered, tonguing her swollen lip. Still shivering. Looking like a little kid now, or someone desperate to be told what to do.

"I'm sorry," I said, rubbing her shoulders for warmth, softening my words. I saw her then as a girl who just wanted someone to pay attention to her, who wanted to be liked by everyone, and I felt bad for her because that's all any of us really want.

"It's okay," she said, making no more effort to slide into me. She looked away, an uncomfortable silence building between us.

"About Caroline," I said.

"What about her?" She sounded spiteful.

"You said you'd tell me something."

Fanny raised one corner of her mouth in a coy smile. "I only said that so you'd kiss me."

"But you know her?"

"I know *of* her. Roger talks about her sometimes. But we've never met."

"So who was with you tonight?" I asked, controlling my frustration, almost sure she was playing with me.

"I told you. Her name is Vanessa." Fanny wrapped her arms over her chest. Looked away again.

"So why did they take off like that?"

"Maybe he was afraid you'd chase him again. Like yesterday."

"I chased him because he ran."

"Why do you hate him?"

"Is that what he told you?" I asked.

She shrugged. "It was pretty obvious the way you looked at him."

"I don't hate him. I just . . ."

How could I explain it to her? Would she understand? Would she even care?

"I just think he's trying to take advantage of the circumstances," I said. "To take advantage of Caroline."

She saw something in my face, or heard something in my tone, that brushed a sudden sadness across her eyes. But it vanished as quickly as it came. "He doesn't seem like that kind of person."

"Did he ever say anything about Pierre? About me?"

"He . . ." She looked away again, shifting uncomfortably. Tried to speak again, but then stopped and started over. "He said you were with him that night. That you . . . he thinks you had something to do with it." Her eyes grew wide and she quickly added, "But I don't think that. I wouldn't be here with you if I did."

Fanny lived a few blocks away. I walked her home. We didn't speak any more, and when the silence became too oppressive, I considered bringing up something meaningless, some idle and pointless conversation to prevent us from drowning in our own thoughts.

And what was I thinking, you ask?

I was right.

Her house was a rundown two-story with blue tile siding shattered in several places. Rain gutters rusted through. One side of the stone foundation crumbling. The unmown grass in Fanny's front yard boxed in by an impotent, waist-high wooden fence missing a number of slats.

I stood there for a minute, not quite sure how to thank her without sounding trite.

Finally, she looked up at me, eyebrows raised in a question, and I knew she was wondering why I hadn't called her after that night at the pizza place. Wondering if it was because of Caroline.

I bent forward and kissed one cheek, then the other, as was the French way.

"*Bonne nuit,*" I said.

And left.

TWENTY-FIVE

I NEVER INTENDED TO hurt Roger. But do you see, now, how it all lines up? Do you see how he'd been turning people against me from the very beginning? First Caroline, then you. And Fanny too, right?

The laptop, open an inch or two, sat on my desk like an indictment when I returned to my dorm. I remembered a day when I was young, twelve or thirteen, playing video games in my bedroom with Dad. I lost—I *hated* to lose—and without even thinking about it, had flung the controller at the television in a fit of rage. The controller shattered into pieces, and took a nice little chip out of the TV screen.

In response, my father yanked down a shelf of cassette tapes and started smashing them. Pulling them out of their cases one by one, snapping them in half, throwing black strings of tape everywhere.

"You want to break your shit?" he'd yelled, cheeks so red and puffed I thought they might burst. "Fine. Let's break your fucking shit!"

I'd cowered between my bed and the wall, bawling, certain that when he ran out of cassettes to break that he would break me next.

I felt ill now, looking at my computer, realizing that a part of me was still just like my dad. I cautiously opened it, not really wanting to see the damage inside.

A jagged, hairline crack ran from one corner of the glass screen midway through to the far edge. A few keys were broken or loose: E, I, V, 5, and F2. The computer hadn't automatically booted, which was a bad sign.

I pressed the power button. Held my breath.

Greenish-red light spilled out from the crack, then spread slowly across to each corner of the screen. For a few awful seconds, long enough for me to compose a requiem for the dying device, the interior fan went quiet and the screen blank. Then it flickered on, rebooted from scratch, and I waited.

My email automatically opened. No longer was the inbox flooded with hundreds of scathing accusations. There was nothing at all from Pierre@Coudreau.net, in fact. I checked the *sent* folder, expecting at least the one message I'd typed up in response, but it was gone too.

Roger had deleted it all.

TWENTY-SIX

CLASSES RESUMED, FOR ME as well as the others who'd had Pierre as a teacher, the next day. While I was in Arizona, the university had given a sabbatical to all of Pierre's students. Time off to mourn or simply pay respect however they chose.

Not surprisingly, Caroline didn't show up to assist the new teacher, a stocky woman with a spot on her upper lip that screamed *skin cancer*. She spoke slowly and quietly, almost too quiet, as if anything louder would be disrespectful to her predecessor's memory.

It hadn't even been two weeks since Pierre's death, and some of the other students were still distracted during that first class back. My thoughts were with Caroline rather than her brother. After sleeping on our encounter the night before —though I suppose *encounter* wasn't really the right way to put it, since she had been in disguise and pretended not to notice me when I called her name—I'd awoken nauseated and wanting to go home. In fact, I had even packed a bag, a suitcase that remained locked and loaded at the foot of my bed, with the intention of buying the first plane ticket I could afford.

But I knew that if you suspected me in anything, I would never have made it out of the country, maybe not even the town. And if you didn't, then I had no reason to leave.

Around six a.m., under the cover of a baby sun, I noticed an unfamiliar car parked outside the Portuguese bakery near my building. A half-hour or so later, showered, dressed, and exiting the building with my language books in tow, I noticed a man leaning into the driver's side window of that vehicle, exchanging a few words, before the driver left.

It didn't concern me at first. New students dropped in all the time. But as I'd walked across the lawn to the faculté, I'd noticed him following me, then diverting suddenly to the ATM. I watched him for a few moments, but didn't see a single bill pass from the machine to his pocket.

I passed the library, floor-to-ceiling plate glass windows revealing lines of bookcases inside and a row of computer tables. I had never seen anyone in there that early before, wasn't even sure if they were open, but there was a woman inside, white hair pinned up in a bun, with a book open in front of her. When she saw me watching her, she hurriedly closed the book, shelved it, and walked away.

And now, while sitting in class, I felt a third pair of eyes on me. In the student parking lot, fifteen or twenty yards outside, stood a man. He leaned against a vehicle anyone else would think was his, but I knew better. He wore faded jeans and an untucked button-down. Casual, but casual like he was working at it. He fired up a cigarette, waved the match out and tossed it to the curb. I stared at him for several minutes, while he smoked the thing down to its butt and then ground the remains under a heel, but no matter which direction he looked, he avoided my gaze.

Did you really think I was so blind, so self-involved, that I wasn't paying attention? Were they watching me specifically, or just watching?

Once class let out, I spent the rest of the day very visible, though self-conscious and sweaty and sometimes forgetting where I was supposed to be next. I felt like young, conceited little Jarrod, who thought that everything revolved around him, that his life story was playing on the whole world's television.

As I stood in line at the cafeteria, I spotted someone about ten people behind me. He conveniently looked away just in time, scanning a poster that denounced another of President Sarkozy's controversial new policies. In the gym locker room, changing out of my kimono after judo training, I caught a guy regarding me from the corner of his eye while he sipped from a water fountain down the hall.

I wished I had taken a French Law class. In the States, I knew, there were measures in place to prevent innocent people from being locked up without a valid reason. Here, I knew nothing. Did you think I would run away? Were you waiting for just that?

It was Roger, don't you see? Isn't it obvious to you yet? He wanted Pierre out of the way, and he wanted me out of the way, so he could be with Caroline.

All I had to do was prove it.

My last session of the day, a conversation class that saw me partnered up with a Scottish girl so proud of her Highland heritage that it was all she spoke about, ended and I was the first person out of the room. I noticed Malcolm McCormack leaning in his office doorway. He raised a hand as if trying to get my attention. I pretended not to see him.

But he's persistent, when he wants to be. And he wanted to be.

"Jarrod," he said, jogging to catch up and amiably tugging at the back of my shirt. "Are you alright?"

His voice shook me with how sturdy and level it sounded. He'd progressed through the stages of grief like a champion.

"You look like hell," he said.

I was clean and shaven, more than could be said about a lot of the French students. Okay, so I hadn't eaten much in a few days, had probably lost a few pounds, but was that so strange, considering?

"Anything I can help you with?" he asked, and the glimmer in his eye was so much different than my mother's when she would ask the same question. She seemed to ask for herself. Malcolm seemed to be asking for me.

"I'm fine," I said. "But thank you."

"I've—" He stuttered, started again. "I've had complaints, Jarrod. I mean, people are concerned about you."

"People?"

"Other students."

"Who?" I said, perhaps a little too tersely.

"You know I can't tell you that."

"What did they say?"

"Someone saw you fighting the other night. During the rugby match."

I showed him my knuckles, which were normally red and callused from training, but weren't now. "Does it look like I've been fighting?"

"They're worried, that's all. I don't think you realize how hard Pierre's death has hit you."

I tried to laugh, but there was no humor there. "You have no idea what Pierre's death has done to me."

"I don't think you do, either. Remember how I was a few days ago? I think it'd help if you talked about it."

"It would help," I said, and meaning it. But just when I was about to ask him if we could talk in his office, he slipped up. He looked past me when he thought I wasn't paying attention.

And I turned in time to see a janitor—if that's indeed what he was—leaning against an office door, watching us. Listening to us.

"Yeah, it would help," I said again. "But who do you think I should talk to, Malcolm? Gerardy? Or all the people he sent to watch me?"

"I'm not sure I—"

"Because it was *you* who sent Gerardy after me, right?"

He shook his head. "Jarrod, I—"

"What did you tell him? That you think I had something to do with it? So it's not only Roger now?"

"No, no. Of course not," he said. And he was back stepping now, looking around as if hoping someone might intervene. "Not only Roger?"

"And why, Malcolm? Is it because I left the day after? Is it because Caroline disappeared? Is it because someone saw me *fighting?*"

Malcolm shivered as he pulled out his inhaler and sucked deeply on it. It had the effect of an alcoholic swallowing his first shot of the morning. Calming, but somehow regretful at the same time. It made me think of my mother. And the way Malcolm looked at me then, I knew he understood. I was trapped in a spiral of self-destruction. He understood because he'd been there, but he made it out. Most normal people do.

I'd been avoiding the reality of Pierre's death. All of this other stuff, the games with Roger and Caroline, the troubles back home, were distractions I'd used to shove my feelings about Pierre way down inside where they couldn't affect me. I hadn't dealt with it.

I left Malcolm, shaking my head and apologizing, because the look of genuine concern on his face almost made me cry.

At the end of the hallway, I turned toward the exit and almost T-boned the janitor. He must have split when I'd noticed him. Now he was pinching coins into a coffee machine, startled that I'd nearly run him down.

Me, of all people. That brought a smile to my face.

"*Pardon,*" I said, squatting to pick up some of the money he'd dropped.

"*Merci,*" he said, taking his change, but refusing to meet my eyes.

I started to walk off, then stopped as if I'd just lighted upon something important.

"In case you're wondering," I said, "I'll be heading downtown in about twenty minutes."

That got his attention, but he still wouldn't look my way. His cheeks flushed a deep red and his fingers froze on the money slot.

When he failed to respond, I said, "The cemetery, if you'd like to come. I have to pay my respects to my teacher."

I strode away, eventually hearing the steady clink of coins sliding into the machine, but as I turned and stole a final glance inside the building, he had gone.

It was the first time all day I'd felt unwatched.

TWENTY-SEVEN

DURING OUR INITIAL TOUR of the city, Malcolm McCormack explained that the Cimetière Urbain was a rather exclusive place. It boasted a few celebrity tombs, costly annual fees. If living relatives failed to keep up on payment, their loved ones could conceivably be removed and replaced by richer corpses. From down the road, it appeared as spectacular—though on a much smaller scale—as the famous Pere Lachaise in Paris, where the tombs of Jim Morrison and Oscar Wilde attracted the most attention. Weeping saints draped upon moss-covered stone crosses. Some of the individual mausoleums were larger and more decorative than my bedroom and my dorm room put together.

Further away from the street, hidden under shades of sycamore, rows of small, flat stones lay embedded in the ground. This was where I found Pierre Coudreau, in an area clearly not prime real estate, with fresh squares of long green grass planted atop him.

I sat down, cross-legged, at the foot of the plot, forearms resting on my knees. There was no epitaph on the stone, no poignant quotation, only his name, birth and death date, the latter of which was barely two weeks in the past.

"I'm sorry," I said, mist collecting in my vision, a dull hollow ache in the pit of my stomach. A young couple walked by, hand in hand, fingers intertwined. I didn't care if they heard me. Cemeteries are one of the few places where you're allowed, almost encouraged, to talk to yourself. "I shouldn't have left."

A shadow fell over me, and a woman spoke. I rose on instinct, twisted up, wiping my face with my sleeve.

"*Qu'est-ce que vous faites?*" She wore a cautious frown, short springs of amber hair swept behind her ears. Both hands curved under the slight bulge of her lower abdomen, which appeared to be the only healthy thing about her. Her cheeks were sunken, and the makeup she'd put on accentuated her pallor. She didn't have the glow pregnant women usually have. Her light was there, but muted and pale, as if the child in her belly barely kept it lit.

"What?"

"*What are you doing on my husband's grave?*" Her accent was soft, like Caroline's, but her voice was hard.

I tried not to stare at her stomach, tried to push away the sorrow leaking into my heart.

"He was my teacher," I said, swallowing tears, my throat hitching. "I'm so sorry."

What a useless, insignificant word. *Sorry.* Looking at Audrey then, seeing pain and anger and a sense of unfairness written all over her scowl, I couldn't think of a word strong enough to express my regret.

"You're sorry," Audrey said. She pointed to a groundskeeper walking by, a man in beige Dickies, twirling a large key ring and humming tunelessly. "He's sorry. The priest is sorry, the university is sorry. Everyone's fucking sorry, and it doesn't mean anything."

"I wish I could have done something," I said.

"Don't they all."

Audrey squatted down over Pierre's stone, swatted away a leaf that had fallen and obscured the name. She said something too quietly for me to hear, then closed her eyes.

"Is there something you want?" she finally said. "Because I'd like to be alone with my husband."

I hesitated, considering whether this was the time or the

place to ask what I needed to know. But I asked anyway. "Do you know where Caroline is?"

Audrey said nothing.

"She left."

"We should be so lucky."

"What?"

"Go to the boulevard. I'm sure she's there with her boyfriend."

"Boyfriend?"

"The drunk Australian?" she said, turning it into a question as if I were either a child or a moron.

"Caroline said she and Roger were roommates," I said.

"Roommates." Audrey laughed. "Are you that naïve? And what do you want with that bitch?"

"To tell her I'm sorry." That impotent condolence again. "Sorry for her family's loss."

And sorry I allowed her to lead me on the way she did.

"Her family?" Audrey stood, pushed me. "Hers? Let me tell you something about *her* family."

Audrey's lips twisted and she stepped back, looking suddenly unsteady, wavering like a dandelion in light wind. She clutched her gut, doubled over. Groaning.

"Get help," she said through clenched teeth. "Please, for God's sake, get help."

I caught her as she stumbled, laying her down atop Pierre's grave where the grass was most fresh and soft, and hollered to the groundskeeper.

"Help is coming, Audrey," I said. "Try to relax."

She squeezed her eyes shut, tiny clear droplets seeping through the lids and down her cheeks. A patch of blood the size of a dime had formed at her crotch, breaking off into trails, spreading like thin red fingers across her slacks.

"You're okay, Audrey." I kept using her name, a calming technique. It created a false bond, a sense of closeness in an otherwise tragic situation. But she wouldn't stay calm for long if I had to yell at the groundskeeper to hurry the fuck up.

He finally came running with a cell phone attached to his ear. He nudged me out of the way, dropping to his knees and propping Audrey's head in his lap. He glared at me as if I'd done something horrible. As if I'd made her bleed.

I stayed with them until the ambulance came, sirens wailing as it backed up to the gates. A trio of men brought a stretcher and carried Audrey away. The groundskeeper went along, his hand tightly clenching hers, leaving me alone at Pierre's grave.

But I wasn't alone. A hazy, luminescent cloud materialized over the spot where the grass had been flattened, the impression of Audrey's form printed there.

The voice in my head was French, it was English, it was real, and it was unreal. "What did you do?" it whispered. *"What have you done?"*

The panic rose so quickly and so forcefully that my heart felt as it was about to explode through my ribcage. I wanted to run out of my skin, but couldn't move. I wanted to scream, but nothing came out. Just a useless, breathless exhalation that made the light, the very atmosphere around me, swim from the darkness creeping in around the edges. Tendrils swirled in the fog above Pierre's grave, coalescing, collecting into shape, a jagged nose broken by force, tracks of dried blood leading to a pair of swollen, purple lips. Wire-rimmed glasses with one lens shattered into a spider's web, and behind them, white eyes filled with such malice that I vanished into them and collapsed and then everything was black.

TWENTY-EIGHT

A CHANGE IN TEMPERATURE, cool wind, hairs raising on my arms like a cloud has passed in front of the sun. Far, far off, car horns and the hydraulic squealing of bus breaks. A wet, earthy smell in my face as I'm clawing my way from some hole I'd fallen into, dirt clogged in my mouth. This feeling in my head like someone had shoved a spike into the soft spot just above my ear.

And my name. At first as distant as a jet engine soaring thirty thousand feet above the ground, then closer, floating on the faint scent of lemon body lotion and laundry detergent.

I opened my eyes, a grueling battle of will that for some strange reason I associated with birth. At first I thought I'd failed, that I was still looking at the backs of my eyelids, until shapes and forms became visible, only outlines, silhouettes, and I realized night had fallen. Above me, I could just make out the sky so darkly blue that it was almost purple, partially obscured by long, thick branches that creaked and rustled and swayed.

"How long have you been here?" she said.

I lifted my head, saw her standing there in those black Adidas trainers and oversized top that disguised her figure. The same outfit I'd seen her in the night before.

Was it the night before?

I groaned and sat up, gingerly, hand on the back of my

neck for support. When I saw Pierre's gravestone, I screamed, a sort of instinctual terror like waking up from a nightmare but still feeling stuck inside it.

"Relax," Caroline said, catching me as I tried to shuffle backward. "What's wrong with you?"

"I . . . guess I fell. Asleep." My throat tasted like dry blood. I grabbed Caroline's ankle, a small exposed area between the hem of her pant leg and her sock. The flesh was warm in my hand, and smooth like a satin sheet so fine it felt almost like nothing. I couldn't let go. I immediately felt guilty for kissing Fanny the night before.

"What are you doing here?" she asked, looking down at my hand, prying away my fingers one by one.

"Apologizing," I said. I had this vague sense of dread, that something terrible had happened and that I was somehow responsible for it, but I couldn't remember what.

"It's about time," she said.

"Am I supposed to call you Vanessa now?"

"That was Roger's idea."

"Was the makeover his idea, too?"

She twisted a lock of raspberry curls in her fingers, and I marveled again at just how much she looked like Jeanette. "It's a wig," she said. "The reporters wouldn't leave me alone. Anyone with a camera and a pen wanted an interview with the *forlorn sister*."

"Why did you run last night? Why didn't you want me to come back?"

"I wasn't ready to see you yet."

"But you were ready to see Roger?"

She sighed. "It was wrong, what I did. I wanted you to know that. I shouldn't have sent you out with my brother."

I blinked. She was assuming responsibility, but her tone implied something else, a truth lurking just beneath her words; that she hadn't believed I was capable of keeping Pierre safe, and that I had proved her right.

"I got him home safe," I said. "Who knows what would

have happened had I not been there."

She said nothing to that, allowing me time to think about my absurd logic.

"I took him home, Caroline. I watched him go into the building."

She looked away, hiding her face. "I blame myself, you know. If you hadn't gone with him, maybe he'd still be alive."

"You blame yourself," I said, stunned. That hurt more than anything she could have said.

"I have to go." She abruptly jogged off, toward the cemetery gates where I had entered, where I was almost certain Roger would be hiding just around the corner.

"Wait," I yelled after her. "You don't know what he's done."

TWENTY-NINE

DEAR J,

EVERY TIME I write you now, the message seems to carry bad news. It's not your father this time, but it is only because of him that we learned what I'm about to tell you.

We had gone to the hospital for his check-up (he's been much better, lately—I know he was a bit more aggressive than usual, a bit quicker to the snap, but that appears to have cleared for the most part), and when they had taken him back for his MRI (goodness, between you and him, I've attended more MRIs in the last few weeks than in my entire life), we passed by one of those small rooms where expecting parents receive ultrasounds? You know which ones I'm talking about? Well, we passed one of those, and for all my life I swore I heard Mario's voice saying something along the lines of, "It'll be okay, there's nothing to worry about."

Now, I had continued on because he has a rather common voice, don't you think? He sounds like any one of a thousand Mexican boys, I would guess, but gosh if it didn't make me think of Mario. But I turned around, Jarrod. I turned around and went back at the sound of weeping. It's a weeping I know I've heard before.

Do you remember when you and Jeanette had gone to the fair up in Tucson, and you'd spent all day trying to win her that silly bear? She told me what happened. You were at school. She'd come over because she needed to talk to someone, and you know that girl's parents—about as useless as a scorpion without a stinger. She told me how you became more and more angry because you couldn't toss the ring onto a bottle or whatever the heck it was, and when she said it was okay, that she didn't want the bear, she just wanted to go home, you grabbed her. She showed me the bruise, Jarrod. But you know what's worse? She stuck up for you. She said it was her fault because you loved her and were just trying to do something sweet for her.

She covered her arm and cried out her tears, and told me to never say a thing about it.

You don't know how many times I wanted to bring it up. How many times.

Anyway, I knew it was her crying at the hospital because that was a sound I'd heard before. Maybe it was none of my business, probably it was none of my business, but I walked right into that room and asked what was going on. Jeanette, poor girl, when she saw me, nearly broke down. Mario took me by the elbow, led me outside, and told me that she was having pains. Bad ones. Well, I didn't have to guess what kind of pains.

But Mario wanted me to pass a message on to you.

"You tell him it's his *fault she's like this. Walking away from her the way he did."*

Now, I'll defend my boy to the death, which is why I tried to never judge you after Jeanette told me the story about the fair. And I defended you against Mario's accusations, too. I told him you have your life to live, and Jeanette has hers, and maybe those lives just aren't meant to be lived together. It doesn't mean it's right or wrong. It just is.

I hope you are well, but maybe it's time for you to think about coming home for good? What is this year abroad doing for you? What is it doing to *you? Is it worth it?*

Your Mother

THIRTY

I RAN DOWNSTAIRS TO the only working pay telephone in the building, followed the directions to make an international call, and dialed home.

No answer.

"Fuck," I shouted into the mouthpiece. I tried Jeanette's house, waited through fifteen rings, maybe twenty. No answer. Called Mario, again no answer. Shouted again into the mouthpiece, then again, and hung up. Picked the receiver up and slammed it down into place twice more.

I went back upstairs, a goggle-eyed local student diverting his path from crossing mine, and typed out a response to my mother.

Is the baby okay? Is JEANETTE okay? WRITE ME BACK AS SOON AS YOU GET THIS. I'm trying to call but no one's home. Anywhere.

My heart pounded in my ears. I read my mother's email again through the crack in my computer screen, thinking between the lines, cursing her for being so vague.

Pains, she'd written. *Bad pains.* Could've meant a thousand things. Not necessarily that Jeanette or the baby were in any imminent danger. Weren't labor pains common? And given my mother's propensity for drama, hopefully she had just made things sound worse than they actually were.

I unzipped the suitcase at the foot of my bed, willing myself to relax, sliding from their rubber sleeves the two bottles of Jurançon wine I'd been planning to give my mother as gifts, but that I'd known I would have drank alone in my bedroom. I uncorked one now, the sweet, sugary sting of white summer grapes in my throat as I swallowed straight from the bottle.

It had been cycling around in my subconscious ever since Mario had told me she was pregnant. I had been burying it, intentionally, pretending other things were more important, things like finding out who killed my sociology teacher and where his sister had disappeared off to and what part Roger Watford had to play in all this, while one little question tugged beneath the surface:

What if the kid is mine?

Of course it was possible. I'd done the math.

But that question inevitably led to another, one I was not ready to answer.

Is that a reason to stay here or go home?

I drank the neck of the Jurançon, wincing at the ultra bitter tang, thinking that I would have done the right thing if I'd found out the kid was mine. Thinking that I *will* do the right thing if the kid is mine.

I took my bottle across the street to the university. The faculté des lettres, where I studied, and all the other buildings had been locked up just after lunch. Students had again announced a strike, this time in defiance of the school's security precautions, or lack thereof. Using Pierre's death as a precedent, and the appearance of his stolen personal items in a trashcan near his office, the strikers insisted they were not safe on campus.

But there was a door around the backside of the courtyard that was never locked, an emergency door the foreign students used whenever the locals pulled stuff like this. I slipped inside, took three flights of stairs up to the darkened computer lab where a couple of people had already laid out sleeping bags on tables. I switched on the machine furthest from the snoring protestors, waited through the blue startup screen of death while finishing off the Jurançon, then logged on with a generic user ID.

"Pierre at Coudreau dot net doesn't exist?" I whispered. "I'll *make* it exist."

I filled out all the necessary information to register a domain name, used my credit card to pay the twenty euro fee, and setup an email account for a dead man.

Roger's address was easy enough to find in the university's database. I wanted to scare him, that's all. Scare him the way he tried to scare me.

But at that point, affected as I was by a bottle of wine and thoughts of home, I couldn't come up with anything clever to write. So I sent him a blank message, then crept out of the building to let the strikers sleep in peace.

THIRTY-ONE

AS THE NIGHT DREW in, I fought the temptation to draw in with it and sleep on all of this, knowing that if I put it off tonight, I'd likely put it off tomorrow night and every other night until I convinced myself that it didn't matter anymore. Pierre would still be dead, no matter how hard I tried to clear my name and my conscience. Roger would win. He'd get away with murder, in a sense, and he'd get the girl. And when I thought about how Jeanette—Caroline, I mean— blew me off at her brother's grave, I spitefully wondered if she and Roger didn't deserve each other.

What about you, Gerardy? How long would you ride me? As long as the case remained open?

But after that initial cold spell—my thought that Roger and Caroline belonged together—passed, I knew I couldn't let *them* happen.

She's in danger, I reminded myself. *No matter what you think of her now, don't forget that.*

But what *did* I think about her? Did I still think there was a chance for us? I'd like to say I wasn't concerned about that, since it was really such a small, insignificant detail in a larger picture. But I was. I'd make her regret choosing Roger over me. The only way to do that was to prove he had killed Pierre.

Was he there that night, when it had all started? Had he been waiting outside Pierre's apartment? I reached back into my memory, playing the whole scene in reverse, ending at the beginning. Caroline and me at the restaurant. Roger interrupting our conversation because he had locked himself out of their flat.

How much had he heard?

I slipped into Roger's perspective and realized how perfectly the whole situation had presented itself to him. He knew we'd be at the bar. He *knew* something would go down, and he *knew* I'd escort Pierre home.

Even as focused as I'd been that night, it'd have been easy for me to miss him in the crowd. Hell, he'd probably been hiding behind hookah smoke, close enough to hear everything Pierre and I were saying.

The son of a bitch.

And how stupid was I for not realizing it sooner?

Had I not kept the address Caroline gave me—had *you* not given me the address back after I showed it to you—I might not have even been able to find the bar again. It was hidden down a maze of alleyways, broken streets so thin I could almost stretch my arms out and touch the buildings on either side. Streetlamps seemed to flicker and fade the closer I came, until the entire road was bathed in a low, sleazy light fitting of watering holes and backroom, third world sex trades.

Outside the bar, as before, I pressed my ear against the door and listened. It was early, not yet eight o'clock in the evening. I didn't want to wait much longer, didn't want to risk running into anyone who was more interested in fighting me than talking to me. The only person I wanted to see was the bartender, the man Pierre had called Brick.

Someone had replaced the red bulb in the ceiling with a black light, throwing purple and white neon shadows across the walls. At the end of the front hallway, I thought I heard the door creak open behind me.

I turned left, without looking back, into the direction of the barroom. A tickle of déjà-vu up my spine as I heard Edith

Piaf again, singing the same song that had been playing when I'd first arrived here.

The room was already smoky—or *still* smoky; I had the impression places like this changed little between daytime and night. I slipped inside, chin low into my chest, looking at everything and nothing. Brick was to my left, his back facing me, standing on a chair and scrubbing a high shelf. A few patrons sat drinking in far corners, but no one I recognized from that evening. No leather jackets. No burly skinheads. A couple of low key businessmen, their ties loosened or stripped off completely, getting their pregame buzz on before heading home to wives and children.

I reeled then, light-headed and suddenly dizzy, when I glanced over at the table where I'd met Pierre. He was there, again, scratching observations into his notebook, every now and then slyly raising his head to take it all in one more time.

Brick turned, acted as if he didn't see me, then went back to cleaning. I leaned against a bar stool, struggling to catch my racing breath and ease the compression in my chest. The air stank of stale tobacco and something stronger laid over it, like rust or copper. Pierre looked up, saw me—my breath *and* my heart stopped for a moment—then went back to his writing as if I were just another drinker. He shimmered in a smoky haze and I rubbed my eyes. It wasn't him. *Couldn't* be him. But I was compelled toward the table as if the person there was pulling a rope lassoed around my waist. Instead of sitting next to him as I had before, I slid across the bench to the very spot he occupied.

A half-empty beer glass sat at my left hand, a half-full journal at my right. My vision fractured, my thoughts. I wanted to weep with the certainty that I was both alive and dead at the same time. As if Pierre had reached his fingers into my soul and moved me like a marionette, I downed the bitter beer, waved for another, then picked up the pencil and began to write.

Everything was in French, including the bits scripted by

my pencil now. My splintered focus understood only selected words, letters were floating, winking in and out of sight, yet I seemed to understand it all perfectly. They were my own ideas and concepts, my own thoughts rippling through in some strange mix of French and English.

Brick replaced my glass with a full one, and tucked a paper receipt under the ashtray beside it, a smoldering cigarette dropping ash onto the tabletop.

"*Merci*," I said.

The pencil marks grew blurry. I pushed my glasses higher up to my eyes.

But, goddammit, *I don't wear glasses.*

At some point, the jukebox skipped and began playing *Je Ne Regrette Rien* over again. The low hum of conversation in the room suddenly stopped, and I looked up to see myself walking through the door.

THIRTY-TWO

MERDE. IT'S THAT BOY who comes into class smelling of wine. Does he think I cannot tell?

I push my face deep into my journal. If I pretend not to see him, perhaps he will go away.

"I'm looking for someone," he says to Brick, and in that typical, too-loud American voice.

Brick, I jot into the margin of an already filled page. *I wonder if he is called that because of his skin color? Man has a tendency to hide insult in humor.*

The boy says it again, but in French this time. Ouf. His accent sounds like the belch of a terminally ill frog.

He sees me, and he sees that *I* see *him*.

Brick says, "You better look with a drink or get the fuck out."

I have made a similar note before, but I add to my journal, *Those lacking in confidence tend to use brash words and volume to intimidate.*

Dear Lord, he's coming this way.

"What are you doing here?" I ask, sucking my cigarette down to its end, exhaling heavily as if I might blow him away.

"Caroline told me you'd be here," he says.

"Of course she did."

Ah, Caroline, my sweet sister. In my journal I write, *I tire of breaking boys' hearts for you.* I hide my words from him, though if I judge from his classroom activity, I doubt he is capable of comprehending them.

"It's not what it looks like," he says.

The little pest sits down next to me, even though I wave him to a chair opposite me. He stares at everyone in the room, and everyone stares back. He attracts far too much attention.

"What does it look like?" I ask him.

He shrugs, drinking half of his beer in one swallow like a barbarian. No taste at all for moderation. No grace, only a desire to alter his own behavior. *Disturbingly common in younger generations,* I write.

"What did she say?" I sigh, gently placing my pencil into the journal's creased binding. "*Buy him a beer, Jarrod. Make friends with him.*"

"Word for word."

I sip the remainder of my beer, wave for another. I sense there may be a long night ahead.

"I'm not going to hurt her," Jarrod says, his accent thickening exponentially with each drink.

"You don't *intend* to hurt her, you mean." I think, but do not say, *If only she took the same care with you.*

"I mean what I said." He narrows his eyebrows at me as if I had questioned his integrity, and begins rattling his fingertips against the table.

"Look around you," I say. He has already finished his first drink and begun on the second Brick has brought. "At least one of these men—more likely three or four—will go home and hit their wives or children. Or both." These are the lessons I try to keep out of the classroom, even though they are often more true than what I teach.

"I'm sure the alcohol has something to do with that."

I wonder if the irony is not lost on him.

"What I'm saying, Jarrod, is that we hurt people. We don't always mean to, but we hurt people. It's coded in the DNA."

I am referring to Caroline, hoping to let this boy down gently. I hope he sees her story reflected in his own.

"You have an awfully cynical view of the world outside the classroom," he says.

"Oh, we are not all sociopaths." I pause to sip from my own glass, noting that I have been here for nearly an hour, and this young American has already drunk twice as much as I have. "Though we may feel remorse afterward, however, does not mean we will not cause pain again in the future."

"So you come to places like this to confirm what you already believe?" He is beginning to slur his words. The stares of onlookers are darkening. I try to quiet him.

You would not understand, I want to say. But I can see he does not want to hear it. He does not want to know about Audrey and the baby that is not mine. He would not understand how much I love her—how much I still love her —even though she is with someone else's child. He would not understand why I forgave her even though she'd caused me so much pain, or why I will raise the child as if it were my own.

So I tell him what he wants to hear because I am too exhausted to do anything else.

"It's a microcosm," I say, dredging up keywords found in any beginner's sociology textbook. "A test subject, *une petite société*, where you can watch a dramatization of the downfall of man in one evening." I try to smile for him, but I feel the gesture is transparent. "And it happens *every* evening. It's fascinating."

Minutes pass without another word between us. Jarrod orders another round, one for me and one for him, but he finishes them both before I have even completed my second drink. There seems to be a dark cloud gathering over him, and though I attempt to write, I notice his lips moving silently. A group in the opposite corner, men who wear the dressings of a motorcycle gang, openly glares at us now, as if our presence alone is an invitation to fight.

Finally, Jarrod looks up and says, "I think we should talk about this somewhere else."

I do not like his eyes. There is something in them hiding just behind the pupils, something more hostile and threatening than the stares of the motorcycle gang.

He will have to leave without me.

"I'm not finished with my beer," I say, with no intent to drink any further.

"Yes you are." Jarrod clutches my wrist, his fingers whitening the skin. "Come on, Pierre," he says through clenched teeth.

I sink into my seat but he pulls at me, laying out a fist of bills for the unpaid drinks.

"I'm sorry for him," he says to Brick, implying that *I* am the drunk and disorderly person here.

"*Aidez-moi*," I shout. Brick or gang, I do not care. Just, someone, help me. This boy is strong, yanking me around like I am a disobedient dog. I twist my arm from his grip, and feel a rush of air beside my face. The room has spiraled quickly into chaos. I don't know who has done it, but someone has crashed a glass into the back of Jarrod's head.

Rather than slow him, this only has the affect of making him more furious. "We're leaving," he yells, as if still trying to protect me rather than assault me, and a man clad in leather attempts to dive past him, to block the exit maybe, but Jarrod is too fast. He trips the man. His friends are nearby. They flail out, attacking him from every direction, leaving me an opening to run past and into the hallway.

Someone has left the door open. The hallway pulses as I hurry through, its light bulb swinging back and forth from a gust of wind that shoots through in vacuity. I don't think my heart has ever beat this fast and my legs are already numb. There is a stitch in my side that is like a dull knife pressed up under my ribs. I flee through backyards and between fences, gasping for air but still breathing, muscles like rubber but still moving, dogs barking all around me, and thank God Jarrod does not know where I live. I only stop when I come to the front door of my apartment building, panting, the air like fire in my lungs.

Audrey is awake when I come inside. She sits on our little white couch eating chocolate ice cream straight from the container. She has scolded me before for doing the very same thing, but she is pregnant, so she is allowed.

"What is wrong with you?" she says, digging the spoon in, but not looking away from the television where a repeat of *Un Diner Presque Parfait* is showing. "I can hear you breathing from here."

"I thought I would go for a jog," I say, doubled over, hands on my knees, swallowing the bile working up into the back of my mouth.

"You hate to exercise."

I wait a moment before responding, until I can speak without stopping. "I have a child to stay in shape for."

She turns toward me then, just her head the way she does, and smiles. Her cheeks flush, eyes sparkle. I do not care, at this moment, who else she has been with.

Audrey returns her attention to the program while I shower, while I decide how to approach Jarrod Nelson the next time I see him in class. If he loves my sister the way I love Audrey, I suppose he could be forgiven for such a passionate outburst.

I will act as if nothing has passed between us. In seeing my example, I pray he will act the same way.

And Caroline will have to deal with her mess. I will no longer be her mouthpiece. I have saved her too many times.

Audrey has moved to the bed when I come from the shower, toweling myself off in front of her. Her eyes are closed, so softly closed that it seems a wisp of wind would open them. She wears a thin white blouse, both hands folded over her stomach, perhaps an inch below her navel, and I have never seen a more poetic picture.

My journal, I remember. In my haste, I left it at the bar. Besides notes for the book I am working on, it contains lesson plans for the rest of the semester. I check the time—it has been an hour since I fled—and quickly dress. I call the police as an afterthought, hoping the motorcycle gang has not seriously injured Jarrod.

I should have called them sooner.

"Audrey, my love," I whisper into her ear, as curved and smooth as a tiny seashell, "I'll join you in a moment." She moans, half-asleep, and purses her lips, and I kiss her before leaving.

At the doorway I pause, turn back, and kiss the hands upon her stomach.

The air has cooled outside, and after locking my door and walking a few steps, I consider returning for a jacket. Something stops me. A sound.

Not something. Someone.

"That was a close call," he says.

It is Jarrod, I know, but I cannot locate the origin of his voice. I squint into the darkness, my sight adjusting and angles sharpening in the moonlight, and then I see him perched upon a fence near the corner.

"I have to go back," I say. I will not show him weakness, nor fear.

"Are you mental?" Jarrod hops off of the fence, holding his hands out against the crossbeam to steady himself. From where I stand, his eyes appear black.

"I forgot my notebook." I swallow. As he approaches, there is more than just alcohol on his breath. I wonder if rage has a smell.

He lunges and grabs the collar of my shirt. "You're not going back for your goddamn notebook." Flecks of spittle spray my face, but I stand firm.

In the distance, I hear sirens. Jarrod tilts his head.

"You called the police?" he asks.

"I didn't want them to hurt you."

He seems shocked by this, pulling back and loosening his grip. "I love Caroline," he says.

"I know."

The boy wells up, tears shining like crystals. I take advantage of the moment.

"Jarrod, Caroline sent you to me because she is a coward."

That gets his attention.

"She is afraid to tell you the truth."

"The truth?" He speaks so low I can barely hear him.

"It has happened before. She has . . . something, I don't know, that men go crazy for. She attaches herself to foreigners because she knows they will eventually leave."

"But I won't leave."

"That's why she sent you to me. Too many times I have done this for her."

Jarrod releases my collar, turning away to hide what I can only assume is shame. "You're saying she doesn't love me?"

Damn you, Caroline. Damn you for putting me through this.

Jarrod faces me then, his cheeks awash. "She doesn't love me?" he says again.

"I'm sorry. No."

For one second, he looks about to collapse. I expect him to fall, and I will try to catch him though I am not near as agile or fast as he. He shows such frailty, such insecurity just then that I feel he will break. Simply snap like a tree limb. But the sadness changes so swiftly to something malicious. I do not even have time to react.

The first strike is more of a shock than anything else. During my observational studies, I have suffered worse at the hands of people much more evil than this boy. But what I see in his face is a hatred so pure it is fantastic. Though it is directed at me, as a sociologist it is hard not to marvel.

"You're a fucking liar," he says, tightening his fist and striking again. My glasses smash against my brow, instantly splitting open the flesh. "You're just like Roger. You don't want me to be with her."

He hits me again. And again. The strikes are coming so fast now, and from so many angles that I am disoriented, and cannot tell in which direction my own front door lies.

"She told me," he yells, as I fall into a crouched fetal position. "She told me you would say something like that."

"That's what she does," I say, or try to, but I can only spit mouthfuls of blood.

I can't think. All I can do is crouch and cover myself with my arms, one of which already feels like it is broken. Crouch, and cover, and say please.

But some sort of shroud has come down over Jarrod's conscious mind, something that eclipses his ability to respond as a normal human being would. Something I imagine is there even when he is not drunk, although I sense he is never entirely in control.

"Please stop," I say, as punches and kicks continue to land and fluids leak from inside my body.

But he doesn't hear me. He is in that space where he hears nothing. I would bet he has been in that space before.

"Please," I say, one final time, "my wife is going to have a baby."

THIRTY-THREE

KNOW WHAT I'VE BEEN working on, Gerardy? Since I'm cooped up here with nothing to do but watch daytime television and eat shitty hospital food, I've been studying my French. Isn't that funny? I've studied more than I did when I was in school, even.

A while ago—and I'm not sure if you even know this—you left a copy of a police report behind. I kept it under my mattress while you visited in the mornings, and worked on translating it after you left. It's strange because I don't remember any of this. It's like reading a story about someone else's life, someone who I know so well but don't really know at all.

For the sake of continuity, I'm going to slip my translation in here so this manuscript will also contain what *you* think happened the night I went back to the bar. Because, let's face it, no sane person is going to believe the story I just told.

Mr. Jarrod Nelson entered [establishment name withheld] at approximately 20:32, according to several witnesses. (See notes attached.) Mr. Alain Gouddard, owner of said establishment, met Mr. Nelson at the bar. What follows is the statement of Mr. Gouddard, while under interrogation as a suspect of attempted homicide.

M: State your name for the record, please.

A: Alain Gouddard.

M: Where were you born?

A: Algeria.

M: What is your current address?

A: [address withheld]

M: That is in Pau?

A: Yes.

M: Are you a legal citizen of France?

A: [silence]

M: Are you—

A: No.

M: Had you met Mr. Nelson before the evening of [date withheld]?

A: Yes. One week before.

M: This would be the same night Mr. Pierre Coudreau was murdered?

A: Yes.

M: And Mr. Coudreau was also at your establishment that evening?

A: Yes.

M: In a previous statement, you had mentioned that Mr. Nelson and Mr. Coudreau appeared to be arguing before they left. About what, can you recall?

A: I didn't understand.

M: In this same statement, you had mentioned that Mr. Coudreau had left your establishment first, while Mr. Nelson remained behind. Is that correct?

A: Yes.

M: Did he remain behind for any specific reason?

A: He was fighting. There were others, all fighting.

M: Approximately how long after Mr. Coudreau left did Mr. Nelson leave?

A: Five minutes. Maybe less. He ran.

M: The patrons were assaulting him?

A: Yes.

M: Were you assaulting him?

A: [silence]

M: Answer the question, please.

A: No. I not assault him.

M: Did either Mr. Nelson or Mr. Coudreau leave any items behind?

A: Yes. A notebook.

M: Anything else?

A: [silence]

M: Wallet or glasses, perhaps?

A: [pause] No.

M: When Mr. Nelson returned a week later, did you recognize him immediately?

A: Yes. I ask him why he want to cause trouble.

M: And what did he say?

A: He say Pierre cause trouble. Not him. I say neither matter. People come to my place for good time, not to fight.

M: But, Mr. Gouddard, hasn't your establishment been the scene of many past melees?

A: Not my problem.

M: But it is, see, because you are the owner, and because you are an illegal citizen in this country.

A: I pay tax.

M: That means nothing, Mr. Gouddard. Let's move on. What else did Mr. Nelson say?

A: [pause] Why I should talk to you?

M: Do you want your family to be sent back to Algeria?

A: [silence]

M: What else did Mr. Nelson say?

A: [pause] He want to know if someone else is in bar with Coudreau.

M: Did he say who?

A: No name. Only that he Australian. With funny accent.

M: Why did you chase him, Mr. Gouddard? Why did you beat him?

A: Like I say, my place is not for fighting.

M: He wanted to fight you?

A: He threaten me. He drunk.

M: What did he say exactly?

A: [silence]

M: What did he say?

A: He say he kill me like he kill the other guy. I chase him in self-defense.

M: With a baseball bat.

A: Yes.

M: You chased him off of your property.

A: Yes.

M: You realize that a plea of self-defense is not applicable in your situation? You cannot 'chase' someone in self-defense.

A: [silence]

M: Do you have anything else you'd like to say?

A: [silence]

THIRTY-FOUR

PIERRE NEVER WOKE UP, but I did. I struggled through a fog of pain and a fire in my head that made me howl when I tried to open my eyes. The lids were gummed shut with what felt like blood. The skin around them puffy and swollen. Somewhere close by, but sounding far away in my head as if shouted from the end of a tunnel, people argued. A woman screamed. A car horn blared.

"She lost the baby," a cautious voice lamented. It was not the Pierre I had just been, nor the Pierre I had known as a teacher. It was not the Pierre who had manifested from my guilt. It was the *real* Pierre Coudreau. The ghost, the lingering spirit, the phantom with unfinished business.

"Audrey—my wife, my love—she was having complications."

I still hadn't opened my eyes. Couldn't bear to see the man leaning over me, grief spelled out in his ghastly face, drawn tight and too old for its time.

"My death, the doctors said. The stress. It was too much for her. She'd begun to bleed, heavily. They induced premature labor. *Four months early.* Do you understand that?"

I nodded as much as possible, lightning flaring up in my neck. Where was I? Not the bar anymore; the way Pierre's voice carried and the shouts of others suggested we were outside.

"She lost the baby," he said again, the tone of lament

replaced with something much more sinister, a lisp, as if he were a snake shooting its forked tongue out as he spoke. "And it was your fault."

Risking further assault or injury, I tried to sit up. The muscles in my lower back gave way, and I crumpled back down. "I'm sorry," I said. I knew how ridiculous it sounded, apologizing to a dead man. "I'm so sorry."

The visions, the hallucinations, the complete mental break from reality or whatever the hell it was that had just happened, it wasn't real. I knew that. The timelines didn't match up with what I remembered of that night. But how could I trust my own memory? Even after all these years, no matter how many times the police had insisted I'd beaten that kid—almost to death—in school, no matter the summer I'd spent in a juvenile detention center in the Arizona desert as a result, I couldn't remember most of what had happened that day in the field outside the lunchroom. From time to time, I even wondered if I had done it at all or if it had been some elaborate setup.

Was this any different?

The shouting grew louder, closer, buzzing in my ears so loudly as to almost eclipse Pierre's final words to me. Almost.

"You took my child . . ." he said.

My eyes flared open and I yelled, a desperate wail completely out of my control. A flash of light and renewed pain. Something—maybe a pipe or metal rod of some sort—came down on the back of my head. I rolled, howling in agony and horror and regret and remorse. The weapon came down again, screams strengthened, and I knew what he was going to say next.

". . . so I took your child."

My view turned sideways as I lay, the taste of spit and blood and pavement on my lips, and I saw there, only fifteen or twenty feet away, Jeanette watching. Her mouth moved, muscles straining as she struggled within the arms wrapped around her waist. Both of them framed by Pierre Coudreau's apartment building.

Caroline, not Jeanette. Caroline with curly, strawberry blonde wig hair splayed from a loose topknot. Caroline with thin, yellow blouse, and shorts that exposed just enough of her legs to make any man's knees weak.

Jeanette, with Mario Nunez holding her back.

No. Caroline, with Roger Watford holding her back.

I rolled my head and saw Brick over me, wielding a metal baseball bat as if he were Reggie Jackson swinging to impress the whites in his first major league game. Veins bulged in his biceps, he twisted and clenched his hands, and I curled into myself, minimizing his target for the next pitch, which I knew was about to be thrown.

Brick tumbled forward, the whites of his eyes huge as someone took him down from behind. They both landed on top of me, igniting a whole new series of injuries from my shoulders down to my knees.

I heard the bat clang against the ground, and everything else spiraled into an oblivion of white noise.

Everything except for Pierre, whispering, "So I took your child."

So I took your child.

So I took *your* child.

THIRTY-FIVE

METAL WHEELS RATTLED AGAINST tile. I shook in my rolling bed as we traveled over bumps and pocks and imperfections in the tile floor. Fluorescent rail lights in the ceiling rendered my eyelids imperfect, transforming them into flimsy lenses I could register shape and substance through. Passing doorways. Waiting rooms where dozing parents rocked their feverish children.

A woman very far away mentioned something about my own peaking fever. Loss of plasma. I understood this even though it was said in French.

We passed a room with a single, occupied, hospital bed. In it lay a woman remarkably similar to the woman Audrey Coudreau had been, only more corpse-like. A fraction of her original size, like a vampire had come and sucked half of the life from her.

She watched, catatonic, as I rolled by.

I didn't ask.

For a while, everything after that came in bursts of vivid activity interrupted by occasional fragments of nothingness. A black mask strapped over my mouth and nose. Intermission. Scissors slicing through clothing. Intermission. The prick of needles and a rush of wind and the surge of powerful drugs racing through my blood.

Then there was one long intermission.

THIRTY-SIX

OUTSIDE THE SMALL WINDOW beside me, snow has begun to fall. It is the first of the season, a swirling mist of flakes like a thousand tiny ghosts, weaving through a labyrinth of tree trunks and jagged, naked limbs. And what if that's exactly what they were, these snowflakes, lost souls or spirits coming back to visit for a while, until the sun shines again and melts them all away?

I haven't seen snow in almost twenty years. It looks like something from a fairy tale.

They tell me I've been here for months. Where is here? A rehab center—though I suspect it's just a politically correct term for Mental Institution—out in the countryside of France. It looks quite like New Hampshire, where I lived until I was four, before moving to Arizona. Lots of rolling hillsides and forests and squirrels and stray dogs wandering around, fur matted because their baths only come when it rains. I suppose it's home now, though I'm not really sure what home feels like anymore.

I've heard fancy words and medical phrases tossed around by the personnel, things like *impulse control disorder* and *schizophrenia* and *PTSD* and *intermittent explosive disorder*, the latter of which, I've learned, is defined by sudden violent outbursts in response to insignificant stimuli. They have me on a number of different medications, but when I ask what the meds are for, they say, always with a smile, "To help you get better."

I suspect the drugs are for anger management. Maybe anti-psychotics.

Understand, even though you visit every day, I'm not always able to talk. It's not that I don't want to—though, most days, I don't—it's because I can't. Either I yelled myself mute that night or my windpipe was damaged beyond repair.

That night.

And though you told me to work at my own pace, ensuring I was always stocked with plenty of notebooks and pens, sometimes the thought of opening a journal is enough to make me sick.

You never came right out and asked me if I did it, and maybe that was because I warned you that my memory was still sketchy. "Write what you can remember," you said. "We'll figure it out in the end."

But I have to say, your unfailing ability to show up every morning, sipping your coffee black with a pinch of sugar, reading what I wrote the day before as the sun crests over your shoulder does not give me hope. And the day I'd finally crawled out of bed with enough energy to walk a few steps, I was even more disheartened to see the detective you had posted outside my door.

I'd written him a note—did he tell you that? Asked him where you were going to send me next.

He'd shrugged, that perennial gesture I had grown so accustomed to, either because he didn't understand or didn't know. I rewrote the question in French, and he said, "*Ça depend.*"

I didn't ask him to elaborate. I already knew. It depended on how the story ends.

At that point, I hadn't even filled a single notebook. Now, there are so many pages I can't count them. I'd started ripping them from the journals, refusing to number them because I didn't even know if they were in the right order. I just wrote things as they came to me.

When you come in tomorrow morning, I might just tell you this is it. This is the whole story. *Then there was one long intermission* will be the final line, and you'll be forced to put the puzzle together with the pieces I've offered you. It's not a very good ending, I admit, but I'm no writer. Just a guy who keeps repeating the same mistakes in life.

There is an ending, of course. There is always an ending.

But it's not always a happy one.

I guess I'll write it anyway. Whether I give it to you is another story.

THIRTY-SEVEN

I WAS VISITED BY three ghosts this week. The first came with my mother. The second came with Caroline. The third came all by himself. That one hasn't left yet.

I don't suspect he ever will.

After Malcolm McCormack had called Mom to tell her I was in the hospital, my condition critical, she'd found herself in a bind. The doctors back home wouldn't let my father fly. They said the chances of him suffering another stroke at such high altitudes were too great. My case was similar. Brick had dealt me some fairly severe head trauma, and I couldn't fly home. Mom had to choose between Dad and me.

She chose me.

She'd arranged hospice care before leaving, and once here in France, called home every day to check up on him. Reports from the nurse were always positive. The only problem was that Dad kept trying to look under her skirt. And that, she said with a laugh, was solved easily enough by just wearing pants.

Mom read everything I wrote too, usually at night, sometimes with me moaning through a nightmare as her soundtrack, so she knew everything before you did. But she never attempted to discuss any of it with me. Once, when I can only assume she'd thought me sleeping, she'd read something that made her bite down on a fist to stifle her cries. She'd dropped the page and gone to the bathroom, returning composed, and slipping the offending page back into place. But I had looked at it while she was gone.

It was the part about Jeanette being pregnant, my fear that the child was mine.

When I saw what had affected her in such a way, my chest nearly caved in. I rolled to my side, my back turned away, and silently sobbed. I heard Pierre's last words, echoing.

"So I took your child."

I sank into a depression after that, not speaking at all to you or my mother. Now and then, mostly at night, when no one was in the room and every square inch of my body felt like it was being flayed with razors, I picked up a pen and considered shoving it into my neck. I wasn't afraid. I knew it couldn't hurt any more than what I already felt.

I finally asked her about it once, when I had dropped into such a state of despair that I thought I might never recover.

"Whose baby was it?" I said, with absolutely no preamble. In fact, that may have been the first time I'd spoken in a month.

Mom's face went white, like someone had pulled a veil over her head. "She wouldn't say. Pretended like it never happened. Jeanette . . ."

She couldn't look at me for a long time. She hid behind her hair and picked at her nails.

"Jeanette moved away. Didn't tell anyone. Just left."

I wondered if Mario went with her, but didn't ask. Did it really matter anymore?

"How did you know?" she asked. She hadn't yet read the climax of my story. I hadn't yet written it.

"You told me in your letter."

"I mean . . . you said '*was*,' Jarrod. 'Whose baby *was* it.'" She looked at me then, lips quivering like a taut rubber band, barely able to contain her sorrow. "How did you know? Did she tell you?"

There was no way I could explain without her thinking me crazy. Maybe, after reading these pages to the very end, she'll understand.

So, for now, I just said, "Yes."

It's still difficult for me to judge the passing of time, but I would guess that Caroline stopped by about a month ago. Only once. She confirmed something I already knew, and revealed a few things I didn't.

"Hello, Jarrod," she said from the doorway, formally, as if I were just another patient. I hadn't been expecting her, hadn't, in fact, ever expected to see her again. Her feet were crossed and she leaned against the jamb, looking like she was afraid to come all the way inside. Looking like she did when I saw her that last night, but without the disguise.

"Hi, Vanessa."

She looked away.

"Sorry."

"What were you doing there?" She moved one foot into the room, crossing the invisible barrier, but stopped there. "What were you doing at my brother's apartment?"

I had been thinking about this very thing, every day, since I woke up from that long intermission.

"I don't know," I said. "I went back to the bar to find the guy who—" The word *killed* stuck in my throat. "—to find out what happened to Pierre."

It was another crazy thing I couldn't explain. Let me try it on for you, and I swear, it fits as snugly as a straight jacket: *I absorbed your brother's spirit and he showed me what really happened. He made me* experience *what really happened.*

I warned you many pages before. Crazy.

But maybe it wasn't what happened at all. Maybe that's just what Pierre wants me to think happened.

"Did you . . ." Caroline said, tiptoeing around the question you had never asked, like she wasn't really sure she wanted to know. Then her features hardened. "Did you do it?"

"Of course," I said, then choked on my words. I coughed until my head hurt, sipped some water from a Styrofoam cup beside my bed, and said, "Not. Of course not."

"Roger thinks you did it."

"Why don't you ask Roger why he broke into Pierre's apartment?"

The defensiveness in my voice did not rattle her. She glared at me and said, "I sent him there to get some of my brother's documents."

"So why did he run when he saw me?"

In a small voice, she said, "Because he's terrified of you."

"Then you should've gone to get the documents yourself."

In an even smaller voice, she said, "Maybe I'm a little scared of you, too."

"It's *him* you should be afraid of. Why don't you ask Roger where he was the night Pierre was beaten to death?" I hated how accusative, how downright nasty this sounded, but there you have it.

Caroline shook her head, said so quietly I almost didn't hear it, "Roger was with me. All night."

She left shortly after. I looked out my barred window to see her walking across a lawn of brown and golden leaves, pulling her coat tight against a rising wind that howled through gaps in the glass. Roger was waiting for her in the parking lot, helping her into a silver car that might have been a BMW or a Dodge Spider. Something expensive. As he circled around to the driver's side, he saw me watching.

I thought he might grin. At the very least, flip me the bird. But he did neither. He simply climbed into the vehicle and drove off.

The third ghost came that same day. He entered with those wire-thin John Lennon glasses perched on his nose, still sporting the same bloodstained polo shirt, and pulled a chair up to my bedside. He sits there writing in his journal, a journal that never seems to be full, though I've seen him turn the page at least a thousand times by now. Every now and then he looks at me, pushes the glasses up the bridge of his nose, then goes back to writing.

But he doesn't speak to me anymore.

EPILOGUE

STEPHAN GERARDY SETS THE pen down, presses his palms hard into his eye sockets. When the blast of static in his vision fades away, he notices dried ink in the webbing between his right thumb and forefinger. The joints in that hand ache; he'd spent all morning on the final report. Six months' worth of details, six months since Jarrod, withdrawn and unspeaking in shock, had begun writing his story, passing pages to Gerardy as he finished them. Sometimes, in a frenzy, the kid would write several in a day. Other times, weeks would pass without a single word committed to paper.

Six months, Gerardy thinks, sinking into his chair. *Has it really been so long?*

He reads that last sentence—*But he doesn't speak to me anymore*—three times, as if such close scrutiny will reveal some new, hidden layer in the story. He glances over at the empty chair beside Jarrod Nelson's bed, and he sees Jarrod staring at the chair with something like patient expectation.

"That is it, then?" Stephan asks in a voice seasoned with Spanish accent, though he'd lived on the French side of the border his entire life. "This is the end?"

Very slowly, as if he has collected all the time in the world and will dispense it as he wishes, Jarrod says, "I don't think I've left anything out."

Stephan nods. "They've convicted the bartender, Monsieur Nelson. Attempted murder. We informed him that a self-defense plea was invalidated when he made a conscious decision to grab his baseball bat and continue chasing you after you left. He accepted the charge in exchange for a lesser sentence."

"So what about me?"

Stephan shakes a cigarette from a half-empty, crumpled pack, and slips it into his mouth. Of course he notices the sign on the wall, the one that reads *Il n'est pas permis de fumer.* Of course he isn't going to light up in a hospital. In fact, he'd quit the habit several years ago, the very day his mother died of lung rot.

But the taste of an unlit cigarette is still divine.

"I'll come back tomorrow," Stephan says, sliding the pages—a couple hundred of them in total—into a leather briefcase. "We'll talk more then."

Jarrod says nothing. He simply returns to staring at the empty chair, suppliant, as if waiting to be told what to do next.

Stephan thinks he may be waiting a long time.

ACKNOWLEDGMENTS

I WOULD LIKE TO thank my family—my mother, Betty, for wanting to read everything I write, even the stuff that makes her stomach turn; my sister, Misty, and my uncle, Mike, for proofing the final draft of this book; and Maria, my beautiful fiancée, for supporting everything I do and feeding my ego whenever it's hungry, but never being afraid to tell me when I can do better.

The Day I Left began as a Master's thesis for Southern New Hampshire University's MFA program, where I was lucky enough to work with several best-selling and award-winning novelists. Particular thanks to John Searles and Craig "Just Fucking Do It" Childs. And I cannot tip my hat to Merle Drown enough—Cap'n Merle helped me take the original, disjointed and largely plotless story (a story I was sick to death of and hated and didn't want to write anymore) and turn it into something I loved so much I didn't want to finish writing it. One novel existed before Merle, and a completely different novel existed after he was done with me.

And to my peers, all the great friends I made in The Program, thank you for the workshops, the late night discussions, the encouragement, the critiques. This book would not have happened without all of you.

DELETED SCENE

THIS SCENE EXISTED IN the first draft (and the second, and maybe even the third), and took place just after Jarrod confronted a pregnant Jeanette at the bakery in Arizona. It contains value, I think, in that it sheds light on a very dark corner of Jarrod's psyche. In the grand scheme of the novel, though, it doesn't fit the overall tone, and it reveals more than I wanted to reveal at that particular point. Further, it delays Jarrod's return to France, which is where he really needs to be. Minor edits and revisions have been done to clean up continuity errors and verb tense, but otherwise, this is how the scene originally appeared.

"You look like a devil has gotten into you," Mario's grandmother said, her cool palms resting gently on my temples. She scrunched her face and those deep leathery wrinkles multiplied, brown cheeks gone bulbous, but her eyes were clear and intense, the bright blue of an infant's on a Hallmark card. "You're so hot," she said, brushing callused knuckles across my forehead, and I thought of my mother saying those same words on the day I came back.

She led me inside the dimly lit adobe home, bending to help remove my shoes at the door, then hooked her arm in mine and walked me down a hallway of messiahs and saints and gods. There were no pictures of her family there, but a hundred Christs with arms corded and pinned out in the same defenseless pose. Fat-bellied Buddhas and pregnant Celtic goddesses. Yellowed photos of Indian sorcerers. Kachina dolls. Mario had once told me his grandmother was a curandera, a shaman, one of the few women who had actually crossed over into—and returned from—the spirit world.

"Come," she said. "I have something for you."

"I have to talk to Mario," I said. "Is he here?"

We passed into the kitchen, from brown shag carpet to reflective white tile, the warm scent of cinnamon and apples seeping through vents in the oven. A small table sat in the middle of the room with balls of colored yarn and twisted sticks piled atop it.

She had been working.

"Is Mario home?" I asked again.

"You're in a dark place, Jarrod." She took my hand and led me out through a screen door. "I see black wind streaking all around you."

The backyard was fenced in, six-foot high wooden slats all around, a mesquite tree with several limbs stretched out like arthritic fingers in one far corner, and in the other, a thatched-roof hut held up with sun washed plaster walls.

I shook my head, exhausted all of a sudden, and not thinking clearly, as if my brain was filled with helium. In all the times Mario and I had kicked soccer balls around in this dust, I had never seen that tree or that hut. But it wasn't right. It couldn't have been. Maybe she'd built the hut only recently, but the tree was old, fifty years at least, its roots sunk deep into the smooth earth around it.

Rosalie—she always insisted we, even Mario, call her by name—pulled a heavy, faded carpet from the entrance and waved me in. I hunched under the low ceiling. The inside was stained black from a fire pit dug into the ground.

"What is this place?" I asked.

She let the carpet fall, but streams of daylight found their way in from unidentifiable locations. They crisscrossed and tangled like string and as I stepped through them, I felt almost strangled by the translucent mesh.

Rosalie's hands pressed against my shoulders, collapsing me down into a cross-legged position. I didn't have the energy to resist. I just sat, watching as she rifled through a cigar box on the other side of the pit. My eyelids were heavy. I blinked, or maybe even dozed or zoned out for a moment, and she was above me, holding a clay-fired mug.

"Drink," she said.

I looked into the mug. "Is it peyote?"

"It's chocolate." She smiled, the lines bunching up at the corners of her eyes.

The drink was bitter, not like chocolate milk or cocoa, but like chocolate baking powder liquefied into sludge.

Outside, the sound of metal slamming against metal. Mario was home. "*Abuela?*" he said. "*Dónde estás?*"

I wanted to call out, but the mixture caught in my throat. I wanted to stand but still lacked the strength.

"He knows not to bother me when I'm in here," Rosalie said, holding a finger to her lips.

I swallowed, grainy backwash clinging to my teeth. "I need to talk to him."

"It can wait. You have a stain on your spirit, and that cannot wait." She struck a match and lit some embers in the fire pit. The smoke that danced upward smelled sweet, like incense. "I'm going to help cleanse you."

She turned back to the cigar box and removed a handful of dark brown mushrooms. I counted six pair as Rosalie washed them, one by one, in a water basin.

"These won't clean the stain," she said, "but they will show you the dirt so that you may clean it yourself."

I took the first mushroom, rolled it in my palm, wondering if I wanted to see those stains. I didn't feel dirty, only confused and betrayed and lightheaded. Seeing Jeanette again had stirred something in me, made me forget about

Caroline for a moment or two. But hearing Mario's voice calling out from the house reminded me why I had to go back. There was nothing for me here. Maybe nothing for me in France except hope.

I chewed up the first mushroom. It tasted like soil, dry and crunchy, making me gag. I choked on four more before Rosalie gave me a sip of water to wash them down.

"Only a sip," she said. "No more."

"Nothing's happening."

"Give it time."

She poured the water basin out over the fire. Flames hissed and threw up steam. The spears of light had vanished, and I was left to finish the rest of my meal in the creeping dark, glowing red embers fading into nothing.

Rosalie began to sing under her breath, her voice soft as a lullaby, some melody carved out of words that weren't English or Spanish. I lay down on my side, suddenly a blink or two away from sleep, and quickly worked through the remaining mushrooms before I passed out. My stomach lurched in response.

"Don't vomit," Rosalie whispered. "The effects will be much more powerful if you keep it all down."

My breath shallowed as I began to see great sheets of dull white fuzz, the static of an untuned station on an old television. I closed my eyes. Opened them. Closed them again. The light behind my eyelids was brighter than the inky darkness inside the hut. The infinite black beyond them was too terrifying to comprehend.

"You're passing through now," Rosalie said. "Don't be afraid." Her voice was distant, an echo of an echo. She started to sing again, louder this time, somehow harmonizing with herself. My chest compressed upon itself and I couldn't breathe, certain that someone else was inside the hut with us.

Then it broke. Just like that. The roof split open exposing the great black hole of a starless sky. I separated from myself, floating upward on a warm breeze that made the hairs on my arms stand up and the back of my neck tickle. Color slowly seeped into the world as if an artist had dumped a bucket of paint onto a three-dimensional canvass. It became all-consuming, and I rose—

fell

—into the sky—

sea

—and raised my arms, laughing, as tendrils of baby blue and purple and crimson spilled over my flesh and dripped from my elbows and fingertips.

And then I came down, as suddenly as I had risen.

From another world, I heard Rosalie say, "You are there. Open your eyes."

I did.

The hut had vanished. So had Mario's grandmother, and so had my clothes. The mesquite tree was still there, just as aged and skeletal as before, but the fence around the yard was gone. I turned around and saw that Mario's house had also vanished. The desert was an oily haze, nothing but shimmering waves of unbearable heat in every direction. I thought this was what the world must've looked like before human life, then I was struck by the idea that I was either the last person on earth, or the first.

I went to the tree seeking shelter, and walked into a mirror of shade. There'd been one tree, and a breath later, there were thousands, millions even, each identical to the next, lining straight through eternity. As if I'd been standing directly at the center point, that place where everything on the other side of the tree was obscured from my vision, and then moved an inch to the right. I looked behind me. The line of trees extended that way, too. From the direction I'd come. My mind reeled at the impossibility of all this, but the grit in my mouth made me remember; this wasn't real.

But if it wasn't real, I should not have been terrified.

I turned back—

forward

—at the sound of whistling. I wasn't alone. Up ahead—

behind

—a man stood facing away from me. I was ashamed of my nakedness, didn't want him to know I was there. My limbs shook with the flood of adrenaline, the horrible thrill of the unknown.

He began walking.

I followed.

He walked in the light, just to the right of the shade provided by the trees.

I walked on the left, in shadow.

And I knew him; the corduroy jacket slung over one shoulder, the loose hem of a blue and white polo shirt flapping from out of his pants. He started to whistle. *Je Ne Regrette Rien*, I recognized immediately.

He stopped, cocked his head, sensing my presence. I could hear his thoughts, a nervous stream of French, and I understood that his fear was stronger than mine.

Pierre turned to me, one of his eyes swollen shut and half of his face peeled away, cracked bone beneath. A flap of skin shrugged off of his forehead with a wet, muddy sound, and I dropped to my knees, vomiting so loudly that I couldn't hear his pleas for help.

From somewhere far away, I heard Rosalie telling me it was okay now, that I could let it all out. I screwed my eyes shut, tears streaking down my cheeks, bile in my throat, and felt her gentle, parchment-like hands brushing sweat from my brow. I jerked away, seeing again the skin falling off Pierre's forehead.

"How long—" I glanced around. It was too bright inside the hut. Rosalie dipped a washrag into a bucket, and then wrung it out over my mouth.

"It's almost dawn."

"Dawn." The word burned coming out. "That can't be."

"The rules of time do not exist in the spirit world."

"It was a trip," I said. "A dream."

She shrugged. "If that's what you prefer to call it."

"I don't believe in the spirit world."

"What you believe doesn't matter."

In a daze, still half in the dream, I felt Rosalie lift me into her arms and carry me inside, an impossible feat since she was three times my age and one-third my size. She settled me into a bed surrounded by windows on all sides, windows covered by paisley curtains that did little to block out the rising sun.

Bathed in hot yellow light, I slept.